Rooted

in Love

Rooted in Love

— an Arcadia Valley Romance —

VALERIE COMER

GreenWords Media

Acknowledgments

I'm so thankful for my fellow Arcadia Valley Romance authors: Mary Jane Hathaway, Elizabeth Maddrey, Lee Tobin McClain, Danica Favorite, and Annalisa Daughety. If you haven't been following the multi-author series thus far, you really need to jump in and check out all the books at ArcadiaValley Romance.com! You'll find the characters behind Delis sausages, A Slice of Heaven bakery, El Corazon, Bigby Farm, and the Arcadia Valley Farmers Market, and if you read *their* books, you'll find references to my characters as well! Start with *Romance Grows in Arcadia Valley*.

A special shout-out to Nicole O'Dell and Elizabeth Maddrey, who gave me a listening ear and bounced story ideas with me when Alaina, Cameron, Evan, and Oliver were a tad uncooperative with story direction. Yes, it happens!

I can't say enough good things about my editor, Nicole, who's been with me since before the beginning of my publishing career. Her keen eye and apt comments are so appreciated, as is her precious friendship.

Thanks to my husband, Jim, who chauffeured me on a road trip to the Twin Falls, Idaho, area in October, 2016, waited patiently while I took nearly a thousand reference photos, and offered his insights of our experiences. I love you, sweetheart. It's you who keeps my love for romance alive.

Thanks to my kids, their spouses, and my grandgirls for their support and interest in my many projects. Special thanks to my daughter who's the cover designer for the entire Arcadia Valley Romance series. It's been fun sharing her expertise with my fellow authors.

I'm always thankful for my fellow inspirational romance author friends at Inspy Romance and my Christian Indie Authors group. I appreciate all who walk the journey with me both personally and professionally.

Thanks to my many readers and fans who've made their home in Arcadia Valley

"It is for this reason that I bow my knees before the Father, after whom all families in heaven above and on earth below receive their names, and pray:

"Father, out of Your honorable and glorious riches, strengthen Your people. Fill their souls with the power of Your Spirit so that through faith the Anointed One will reside in their hearts. **May love be the rich soil where their lives take root.** May it be the bedrock where their lives are founded so that together with all of Your people they will have the power to understand that the love of the Anointed is infinitely long, wide, high, and deep, surpassing everything anyone previously experienced. God, may Your fullness flood their entire beings." (Ephesians 3:14-19 The Voice)

Thank You, Jesus, my Redeemer.

Books by Valerie Comer

Arcadia Valley Romance Novels

Romance Grows in Arcadia Valley
Sprouts of Love
Rooted in Love
Harvest of Love

Farm Fresh Romance Novels

Raspberries and Vinegar
Wild Mint Tea
Sweetened with Honey
Dandelions for Dinner
Plum Upside Down
Berry on Top

Riverbend Romance Novellas

Secretly Yours
Pinky Promise
Sweet Serenade
Team Bride
Merry Kisses

Urban Farm Fresh Romance Novels

Promise of Peppermint
Secrets of Sunbeams
Butterflies on Breezes
Memories of Mist
Wishes on Wildflowers

Christmas in Montana Romances

More Than a Tiara
Other Than a Halo
Better Than a Crown

Chapter 1

CAMERON KRAUS GAZED down the long petal-strewn grass aisle between rows of finely dressed guests seated in padded folding chairs. A mass of tall rhododendrons, loaded with pink blossoms, blocked his view in the distance, while mounds of flowers poured out of urns around the periphery. The fragrance nearly gagged him.

The wedding of the year, reported the Valley Times. Maybe not quite that, but likely the wedding of the month, at least. That's what happened when a long-standing wealthy Arcadia Valley family planned nuptials. Even Grace Fellowship wasn't big enough to hold everyone. They'd had to reserve the park.

He forced his hands to hang at his sides. No fiddling with the cuffs of his tux or adjusting the cummerbund. No shifting from one patent-leather shoe to the other. Definitely no looking at his mother seated in the front row.

Music swelled from the string quartet off to one side as a

bridesmaid carrying a humungous bouquet strolled around the rhododendrons and down the long aisle wearing a royal blue dress that swished around her knees. There was money in the flower and garden center business. No doubt about it.

The matron of honor appeared next, but Cameron's eyes were trained on the gap in the bushes behind her. The violin solo went on longer than during rehearsal, but maybe that was his imagination.

Two little boys in black tuxes strutted into view, each carrying a painted sign. Both smiling.

Cameron dared to breathe. After the near tantrum this morning, he hadn't been sure how the day would play out.

The redhead — his son Oliver — pointed straight to the front and then at his sign. *Just wait until you see our Aunt Jonah.* The other twin, Evan, showed off his placard to the guests lining the aisle. *Don't worry. We're still single.*

Guests chuckled. Cameras snapped. Beaming, the boys soaked up the limelight.

Cameron glanced at his mother just as the music segued into the traditional bridal march. She smiled at the boys as they passed her, but her lips looked tight. She'd told Cameron the boys were undisciplined. Unruly. Needed a firm hand. Maybe now that she and Dad were in Idaho for the summer, she could help him get control of his hooligans.

Hooligans, indeed. The six-year-old twins ran up to him and stood, one on either side.

At the back, the bride made her entrance on the arm of her father. Traditional. Just how Cameron liked it. Eight years ago, Lisa had insisted she was her own woman and strolled down the aisle by herself, much to his mother's horror. He should have known right then and there it would never work out. There'd been clues even before that. Clues he'd ignored.

Standing in front of him and facing the audience, Evan fidgeted. Cameron gently rested his hand on his small son's shoulder. Oliver turned to his brother and stuck out his tongue.

"Boys..." Cameron growled under his breath.

Evan shifted away from his touch and looked up. "How come there's so many flowers?" he blurted out. "I'm going to sneeze."

"Shh. Just squeeze your nose."

A few people tittered. From the front row, Cameron's mother raised her eyebrows and glared at her grandsons.

Right, Mom. Children should be seen and not heard. I remember the drill.

But his sister had insisted the boys take part in her wedding, though no one was crazy enough to entrust them with the rings. Beside Cameron, the best man, Ben Kujak, shot him a sympathetic grin. On Ben's other side, the groom stood focused on his bride. On Cameron's sister.

Joanna — Jonah to the twins — might be two years older, but that didn't mean Cameron figured it was okay for her to get married, although Grady Akers was a decent enough guy. It was just that Cameron liked having his sister living in his basement suite, helping out with the boys after school, cooking dinner a few nights a week. The best parts of having a woman around, with none of the pain Lisa had inflicted in their short marriage.

Cameron angled a glance at Grady. Had he looked this

besotted when Lisa had come toward him? Had Lisa worn the look of adoration Joanna directed at her groom right now? He didn't remember it, but they must have been that in love once. According to his ex, he'd always been too controlling. Too smothering. He hadn't seen it that way. He'd only tried to look after her the way his parents had taught him.

"Who gives this woman to be married to this man?"

Evan sneezed three times in quick succession, and laughter rippled across the gathering.

Cameron didn't need to pat his pockets to know he had nothing to catch the drips. Darn tuxedo.

"Her mother and I do," Dad intoned as Mom ducked low and pressed a tissue into Evan's hand, glaring at Cameron.

Right. His fault again. Everything was.

"When I get married, there's gonna be no stinky flowers." Evan sneezed again.

Oliver turned to his brother. "I'm never gonna get married. Girls are yuck."

"Boys," Cameron whispered, infusing threat to the words as he tightened his grip on two small shoulders.

Once again, all eyes were on them. Now Dad's accusatory glare joined Mom's. Other guests looked less indulgent than a few minutes ago.

Why had he agreed to stand up for his sister and Grady, let alone conceding when Joanna begged him to allow the boys to take part? Not as ring bearers, but in any role whatsoever? He'd figured it would be easier to keep an eye on them if they stood beside him.

"When can we go play?" begged Oliver, looking up at Cameron.

Never. Not in rented tuxedos.

∽ℓ℮

"Don't touch!" a woman called as a man yelled, "Look out!"

Alaina Silva turned toward the voices as the extravagantly tall wedding cake teetered. She caught her breath. The groomsman dashed closer and steadied the table before it went over.

Whew. Disaster averted. Dad didn't keep a spare wedding cake in the cooler, and the staff at his country club had plenty to do for this reception without cleaning up a massive cake spattered across the tile floor.

The groomsman's hands gripped the shoulders of the small sign-bearers as he bent over them. His lips moved as he spoke first to the blond then the redhead, both of whom scowled back at him. Alaina's mom had whispered during the wedding that he was the bride's brother and tut-tutted that he had his hands full with those two rascals and no wife.

As an early childhood educator, Alaina had met her share of single parents and messed-up kids. She'd been able to instill stability into some of those families. Help the children cope and become happy well-adjusted members of society.

She sidled closer, her need to fix things overwhelming her common sense. "Hi, I'm Alaina. Would the boys like to come with me? There's a playground out back. I can watch them until they're needed back in here." Although... the boys wore miniature black tuxes. At least they weren't white.

The man straightened and narrowed his gaze at her. "No, that's fine. They can stay with me."

An older woman stepped in front of Alaina. "Come with Nana, boys. We'll go sit down and wait quietly." Her voice held a hint of a British accent.

The man's jaw clenched. "I'm sure Joanna needs you, Mom. I've got the twins. You don't need to worry."

"I'm only trying to help."

"I know, but it's okay. Really."

The boys exchanged a glance then, as one, ducked free of their father's hands and darted for the door.

"Cameron..."

He shook his head and dashed in their wake, leaving Alaina with the disgruntled grandmother. Um, no. She was so out of there. "Excuse me, please." But where? Out the door. Too bad it wasn't the one to the playground. She bolted after them.

The boys headed straight for the fishpond. Short of falling in, they couldn't get in too much trouble.

"Look, Dad. Goldfish!" One of the little guys leaned over the low wall of stacked volcanic rock.

Not there! A golf cart had rammed that spot just last week, and the rocks were loose. Her father had hired a mason to come in Monday to repair the stonework where the cement had cracked away.

As if in slow motion, the little redhead tipped headfirst into the pond, taking several rocks with him. The resounding splash seemed an after-effect.

"Oliver!" yelled his father.

Alaina sprinted for the pond. Those years of lifeguarding

to pay her way through college surged to the surface, and she reached for the child just as his father did. Between them, they hauled him out of the water.

"That was *awesome*," breathed the other twin.

Cameron pivoted, yanking the waterlogged boy out of Alaina's grasp. "Don't you dare, Evan. I mean it."

Oliver coughed and struggled in his dad's arms.

Okay, whew, he was going to be all right. Other than two soaking tuxedos.

The father crouched and stood the child between his knees. "You okay, Ollie?" His voice sounded strangely gentle, all things considered.

"I'm okay, Dad. The rock broke. I was trying to be good, I promise."

"I know, buddy. Just... you two *have* to settle down. You don't want to ruin Aunt Jonah's special day, do you?"

Both little heads shook.

"There are probably towels in the clubhouse. Want me to go look?"

Cameron looked up at Alaina with a surprised expression on his face. He'd obviously forgotten her presence. "I'm sorry. You started to introduce yourself earlier...?"

"Alaina Silva. My parents own the country club. They're old friends of the Akers family. It's your sister who's the bride, right?"

He rose, fully looking at her now.

Good thing she was all dressed up. She'd been her own sister's maid-of-honor just last weekend in Spokane and drawn the attention of several of Adriana's single guy friends in this dress, so she'd figured why not wear it again. This shade of green suited her, and the style was flattering.

"Pleased to meet you. I'm Cameron Kraus. Yes, my sister, Joanna, is now married to Grady Akers." He gave a rueful shake of his head and held out the hem of his formal jacket. "I think it will take more than a towel to fix this. I need to take the boys home so all of us can change. Yes, Evan, you, too. I won't make you stay in that tux if Ollie and I get to wear something else."

"Yes!" The little guy pumped his fist.

"Still Sunday clothes. No shorts and T-shirts." Cameron's gaze hadn't left Alaina's face. "Do you think there's enough time? We live just a few blocks from Grace Fellowship. It will probably take me half an hour to get there and back."

His eyes were clear and brown and seemed to go on forever, like a well of dark coffee. His brown hair, not much longer than a buzz cut, didn't look like it would muss if a woman ran her fingers through it.

Alaina took a step back, unable to look away. She shouldn't be thinking things like that, even though Mom had said he wasn't married. He was either divorced or widowed. Just because she liked kids didn't mean she should think twice about a man who had some. Bad idea. Really bad idea.

Still, no matter how her brain screamed at her eyes to look away, she couldn't do it. Wait. He'd asked a question. She cast her memory back over the past few minutes.

"It's not a sit-down reception, so I'm sure you'll be back before they cut the cake. It will be pretty casual for a while."

Cameron glanced toward the clubhouse then back at Alaina, a rueful grin softening his face. "I honestly don't want to face my mother right now, but I hate to ask you to let her know where we've disappeared to."

Alaina touched his sleeve. "Don't worry about it. I don't mind."

"Are you sure? She can get pretty... intense."

"I noticed." Alaina smiled up at him. "My mom's no walk in the park, either. I can handle her."

"It's just that my parents don't really know the twins. They live in England and only pop through for a quick visit every year or two. This time they're here for—" his eyes closed for an instant "—another ten weeks. Not that anyone is counting."

"I'm sure she means well."

He shook his head. "I'm sure she does." But he didn't sound like he believed it. Cameron's eyes widened, and he whirled. "The twins."

"Over there." Alaina pointed the opposite direction, where the blond — that was Evan, right? — climbed onto a golf cart.

"Evan!" bellowed the boy's dad. "Oliver! Get over here right now."

Alaina grinned. This was a man who needed eyes on the back of his head more than most. She rested her hand on his arm. "Get them changed. I'll make sure they hold the festivities for you."

He stared at her fingers before his covered them with a light squeeze. "Thanks. I owe you one." Those gorgeous eyes looked deeply into hers for just a few seconds. Then he took the boys' hands. They cavorted beside him as they rounded the building toward the parking lot.

Alaina straightened her shoulders and touched the back of her hand where his warmth lingered as she turned back to the clubhouse. And looked directly into the unsmiling face of Mrs. Kraus.

Chapter 2

"WHAT ELSE DO YOU want to eat?" Cameron leaned low over Evan's shoulder to block the din of voices.

"Some of those." Evan pointed at canapés that looked like they might have egg on them. "And can I have some peppers?"

Cameron stared. "But they're vegetables. You hate vegetables."

The little shoulder shrugged. "I like licking dip off them."

Far be it from him to argue. "Okay. Here you go. How about you, Ollie?"

Oliver pointed out a few items from the long table, including carrots and cucumbers. Cameron glanced around. His sister would want to know about this breakthrough, but then he remembered she was kind of busy at the moment, wandering among the guests with her hand tucked in Grady's. Joanna's big day.

"Hey, Cameron. Can Evan and Oliver sit with me?"

Maisie's brown eyes peered up at him. Last summer he'd

harbored a brief hope that Maisie's mom might fall in love with him but, no, Ben Kujak had won Evelyn's affections. Maybe Cameron had only wanted to make her life easier. Maybe he'd only wanted Maisie as a built-in babysitter. At eleven, she was one of the most engaging and resourceful people he'd ever met. It didn't hurt that the twins adored her.

He nodded. "Sure. Where shall I take their plates?" Because he certainly wasn't entrusting fine china into their little hands.

"I'm sitting with my parents over there." She pointed, and Evelyn waved.

"You calling Ben Dad now?" Evelyn and Ben had been married back in January, not seeing any reason for a long engagement.

"Yeah." Maisie beamed up at him, one arm slung over Oliver's shoulders as they crossed the clubhouse. "He's pretty cool."

"That's great." He even meant it. The tinges of jealousy were long gone, along with any hope that there was someone out there who'd love him enough to take on the twins. Not with the trail of destruction those two left in their wake. They'd scare off any sane woman.

Not that Lisa fit the description of sanity, exactly. What woman walked out on her husband and three-year-old sons? Cameron could see so many ways he'd gone wrong in their brief marriage, but that didn't excuse Lisa's affair with his best friend.

"Hey, guys." Ben scooted out the chair beside him, and Evan dropped into it. "How's it going, Cameron?"

Cameron shook his head, meeting his friend's gaze. "You

don't want to know." He set the boys' plates on the table. "Let's just say males of the Kraus family aren't much for formal affairs."

Evelyn chuckled. "I heard about the unauthorized swim. I bet you haven't eaten yet, either, Cameron. Go get something for yourself. You're welcome to join us, but if you want a break, go for it. The boys will be fine with us for a while."

Hope bubbled. "You sure?"

Ben nodded in agreement. "Absolutely. Maisie will make them toe the line." He grinned at his stepdaughter, love shining from his eyes.

"Thanks. There are a few relatives in attendance I haven't seen in a while." He'd avoid any who were talking to his parents, but he'd never say that in front of the twins. He pointed a finger first at Evan then at Oliver. "You guys be good, okay?"

Two pairs of innocent blue eyes peered back. Right. Cameron knew better.

"Alaina! It's so good to see you." Pretty in pink, Kenia Akers, sister of the groom, threw her arms around Alaina and nearly lifted her off the floor. "I was so excited to hear you got the job at the Grace greenhouse and have moved back to town. When can we get together and catch up?"

Alaina hugged her childhood friend back. "Soon, I hope. I start work on Monday, and so far I've only had a brief tour of the facilities."

"Everyone's been working so hard to bring my granddad's old house up to spec. It needed a lot of renovating to turn it into a daycare center." Kenia clasped her hands together. "Do you remember that dreamy Drew Harrison?"

The brooding bad boy from the proverbial other side of the tracks had been a couple of years ahead of them in school.

"Drew has his own renovation company now, and they did a terrific job on the old house, don't you think?"

Kenia didn't give Alaina a chance to reply before leaning in closer. "Did you hear he and Katie Groves — I mean Kate — got back together after all these years? She moved back to town last summer when her father died and left her the house and the farmers market."

"No, I hadn't heard. Good for them." Katie and Drew had been an item all through school but, after graduation, she'd up and moved clear to Atlanta and never returned. Alaina scrambled to keep up as Kenia kept going.

"Speaking of reunions, did you hear about Molly Abbott and Javier Quintana? They're back together, married in March. In fact, there are so many people falling in love around here, I'm starting to wonder what's wrong with me." Kenia's gaze took in Alaina's ring-free hands. "Anyone special for you?"

This was a fine time for Kenia to actually pause for a response. "Um, no. There was, but we... broke up."

"Aw, I'm sorry to hear. What happened? If you want to talk about it, that is."

Seemed like telling Kenia was a short cut to an announcement in the Valley Times, but what did it matter?

"He was two-timing me. I dumped him when I found

out." That had been over six months back, but it still burned. One of Alaina's friends had seen Garth and another woman coming out of a movie theater. Kissing. And not the kind that could be misinterpreted from the video Nikki had taken on her phone. It had been a full contact sport that had gone on for some minutes.

"What a jerk."

"Yeah." Alaina shook her head. "Anyway, what about you? Dating?"

"On and off." Kenia shrugged. "Maybe I'll stay single and devoted to my career forever. It worked for Aunt Irene. Maybe I'll take over not only her bookstore, but also her role in the town as auntie to everyone."

Alaina glanced around the affluent crowd mingling in the clubhouse. How many of these people had she once known? She hadn't tried to keep up — she'd been glad to get out of Arcadia Valley as soon as high school was over. If Garth hadn't turned out to be such a jerk, she might still be living in Nampa, even engaged to be married to him by now. Although, the preschool she'd worked at had been caught in a power struggle over funding, and the past year hadn't been that much fun, even before adding in Garth's betrayal.

For better or for worse, she was back in Arcadia Valley, at least for a year. Enough time to either settle back into her hometown or know she needed to move on again.

For better or for worse. Interesting thoughts on the heels of a grand wedding. Not far away, Grady and Joanna still chatted with guests. The bride tipped back her head and laughed. The groom watched her with so much love shining from his eyes that Alaina's breath caught.

"I know, right?" whispered Kenia. "I think being single is great until I see what love looks like. Then it kinda makes me want some of my own."

Alaina turned away. "Yeah. Two weddings in two weeks is enough to make anyone into a sappy romantic. My sister got remarried last week."

"Oh, I'm so happy for her. Her first husband died in the line of duty, didn't he? A few years ago?"

"Yes, he was a firefighter. It's been tough for Adriana raising two kids alone, but Myles is pretty awesome. I think they'll do well together."

Raising kids alone. Alaina couldn't help looking around for Cameron. He and his boys sat at a table not far away with the couple who'd been best man and matron of honor. She poked her chin their direction. "What's his story?"

"Cameron Kraus? His wife left him and the twins two or three years ago. He's got his hands full."

Alaina chuckled. "I noticed. Those boys seem to ricochet from one escapade to the next without pausing for breath."

"They're really something. Pretty sure you'll have them in your summer daycare at the greenhouse. Cameron works for Stargil, and childcare has been one of his biggest issues since Lisa walked out."

A man whose wife left him couldn't be that much of a catch. Not really. *You're not back in Arcadia Valley to find romance, girl.* She knew that. But the man was really good-looking and those boys were endearing. Wild, but endearing.

"Tell you one thing, though." Kenia lowered her voice. "Cameron's come a long way. He was a Christmas-and-Easter Christian before, but he's rededicated his life to the

Lord and is really focused on being a godly father now. It's cool to see."

Alaina shot Kenia a glance. "Interested in him?"

"Me?" Kenia's head shook even as her startled eyes swung to meet Alaina's. "Not on your life. You can have him."

"I don't think so." Alaina chuckled. She'd admired her new brother-in-law for taking on her sister's kids. Violet, especially, was a headstrong child who could rival Cameron's twins. Alaina cringed to think of them ever joining forces, though her niece was a year or two older.

Cameron rose from the table, and his gaze swung to meet hers.

Although... she could get lost in eyes like those.

He started toward them, wending his way between other guests.

"I'm out of here," whispered Kenia. "Must be nearly time to cut the cake or something."

Alaina stood rooted to the floor as her friend slipped away. Surely Cameron wasn't seeking her out. They'd had that moment by the pond, but... he looked right into her eyes.

"Care to dance?"

Time stood still. Would she agree? Or would she laugh and turn away? Cameron held his breath, captivated by her brown eyes.

He hadn't danced since his wedding with Lisa. Maybe a couple of times after. His parents had disapproved of it even then, and nothing had changed. They'd likely thought they'd raised Joanna better than they had him, but Joanna had eventually convinced Dad there'd be a father-daughter dance tonight. That was further than Cameron had gotten with Mom eight years back.

The band struck up and guests cleared to the sides of the large room to make way for Joanna and Grady's slow waltz. They'd taken ballroom lessons over the winter and tried to convince Cameron to join as well. Aside from needing a babysitter too many evenings, he hadn't wanted to be paired off with random single women for the lessons, so he'd declined.

Now he wished he'd gone as a refresher.

"I'd like that."

Had he heard her correctly? The air seemed to be buzzing a little, but she was looking up at him. Smiling. Not bolting like Kenia had done. Not that he'd ever given Kenia more than a second thought, even when she'd been the twins' Sunday school teacher last year.

Joanna and Grady took to the floor, all those lessons paying off as they held each other close and swung to the music.

"Your sister is very pretty."

"Not as pretty as you."

Alaina's eyes widened slightly.

Man, had he said that out loud? But it was true. Joanna had appealing features, he supposed, not that a man really noticed those sorts of things in his sister. But the woman beside him, waiting for their turn on the floor? She was the most beautiful woman in the room. There was just something about her long eyelashes framing those enchanting brown eyes. Those brown curls pinned with a clip then cascading down her back. The calf-length green dress that gently hugged her curves. He'd soon know whether the fabric was as soft as it looked. How she'd fit in his arms.

A moment later Grady whirled Mrs. Akers in circles around the awkwardly swaying pair Joanna and Dad made but, hey, at least Dad was making an effort. And then the music changed again and a few dozen people swarmed onto the floor.

Cameron dipped his head and held out his hand. "Shall we?"

Alaina fit against him just as perfectly as he'd known she would, the top of her head tucking just under his chin.

This was either the best thing he'd ever done or the stupidest mistake he'd ever made. Though it would be hard to top Lisa.

Chapter 3

THE CLOSING SONG echoed in Alaina's mind as she gathered her purse and her Bible at the end of the church service. She'd missed worshiping at Grace Fellowship in the years she'd been away from Arcadia Valley.

Rooted in God's love. Pastor Ivan's sermon had reminded her that if her roots were deep in God's word, she'd be equipped to withstand the storms life offered up. That raised the question: would she have gotten so messed up with Garth if she'd been taking her spiritual growth more seriously in Nampa? She hadn't gone her own way. Not precisely. But she'd been complacent. She'd gone to church... most weeks. She'd read her Bible and prayed... some mornings.

"Want to do something this afternoon?" Kenia leaned closer then grinned. "Or are you seeing Mr. Tall, Dark, and Handsome today?"

Alaina knew exactly where Cameron had been sitting across the sanctuary, but that didn't mean she was running over there. How was she supposed to greet the man she didn't know, but had danced with half a dozen times or more? Even now, if she closed her eyes, she could hear the music, feel his arms around her, smell his cologne.

She blinked. "My parents weren't very impressed last night," she confided as they made their way out the door into the June sunshine.

Kenia's eyebrows rose. "It's none of their business, really. You're a grown woman. Twenty-eight."

"I know. But still. I'm living with them until I find a place of my own."

"I've got a two-bedroom cottage down near El Corazon. I could use a housemate. What do you say?"

"Really?"

"Really. I promise I won't get after you if you go dancing with Cameron." She winked.

"Tempting. Not that I think clubbing is going to be my new Saturday night activity. Pretty sure Cameron's parents were glaring at him, too."

"Oh, good grief. My dad is too busy with the garden center — and Mom with Blossoms by the Akers — to interfere in my everyday life. We're not eighteen anymore, Alaina. We've been out on our own for ten years. They raised us to become adults, make responsible decisions, and raise families of our own."

Alaina poked her elbow into her friend's ribs. "And yet you danced with at least eight guys last night. How come you're still single?"

"Haven't met Mr. Right." Kenia held up a hand. "And Cameron definitely isn't him, not for me. He's a bit too old-fashioned, for starters. Plus, I don't want to be saddled with some other woman's kids. I'm sure you've thought about that since yesterday."

"Yeah, I have. My sister just remarried, and my parents tell everyone how wonderful Myles is, and how brave to become a stepdad to Adriana's pair. That's after they got over my seven-year-old niece telling everyone how much she hated Myles."

"Yikes. That's tough."

"Well, Violet adores him now, which helps all around. The thing is, I know it's different. Adriana's husband was a firefighter who died in action over five years ago…"

"And Cameron is divorced."

"Yeah. I get that it's not the same thing. I mean, I don't know anything about his ex-wife. Whether she has partial custody of the boys, or anything. For all I know, he might still be in love with her and hoping to re-unite his family. Wouldn't that be the best thing for Evan and Oliver?"

"I can fill you in, and the answer is no, it wouldn't be best. Not unless Lisa did a complete about-face. She not only walked out on Cameron and the twins, but she did it with his best friend and co-worker. Within a few months she'd ditched Kyle, too, and was on to some other man. She's gone totally wild."

"I never even thought of it that you might've known her."

"I didn't. Not really. But the scandal was big for a town the size of Arcadia Valley. It was only after Lisa left that Cameron started coming to church regularly. He's in my brother's men's group, not that Grady will admit what the guys talk about. But yeah, Cameron's changed a lot since those days."

Last night Kenia had said it had been two or three years. Was that long enough?

"I had the twins in Sunday school last year. Oh. My. Word. What monkeys." Kenia chuckled. "That might have something to do with my lack of romantic interest in Cameron. Besides, he's the Mr. Darcy type. Brooding."

"Sure didn't seem like it last night." He'd been as drawn to her as she was to him, hadn't he? Or he wouldn't have monopolized every dance then asked for her phone number.

Kenia nudged her. "Sometimes it just takes the right woman to turn a man around."

Cameron wasn't Garth. He'd been at the receiving end of the kind of deceit and pain Garth had dished out to her, only more so. He wasn't capable of turning the tables and inflicting the same.

The memory of the morning's sermon niggled. She should probably take time to get her spiritual life in order before dating again. Wasn't that what she'd decided during the closing hymn? But it had been seven months since the breakup with Garth. It wasn't like she was on the rebound. Nor was Cameron. Besides, Kenia said he was a dedicated, growing Christian, so there was no real reason to hold back.

She could grow as a believer at the same time as seeing where a relationship with Cameron might go. The two weren't mutually exclusive. And it might go nowhere. They'd only just met, after all. Why not explore their attraction and see what happened?

"Hey, were you serious about a roommate? Can I have a look at your cottage? Getting out of my parents' house sooner rather than later sounds like a good idea."

"You don't need to put the boys in daycare, Cameron. Why do you think we're here this summer?"

It was Sunday evening, and Mom had managed to contain herself until the boys were in bed. He was seriously going to regret having a basement suite before his parents returned to England in late August. He already did, and they'd only been here a few weeks. Ten to go.

He braced himself. "It's not a problem. I've had their names on the list for so long now I don't dare give up their spaces. I'm not sure when there might be another opening. Arcadia Valley has a shortage of childcare." He'd discovered that in a big fat hurry the day after Lisa flounced out the door.

Mom pursed her lips. "I feel guilty that you're spending so much money when your father and I are right here and well able to take care of the children. Right, Wilfred?"

Dad tapped his pencil against the open newspaper and glanced up. "What's that, Nora?"

"I said we can take care of the boys, and Cameron doesn't need to pay for daycare."

"Right, right. Would do the little rascals some good."

Cameron's back stiffened of its own accord. Not that the twins were easy to deal with. Far from it. But his parents' brand of discipline wasn't anything he wanted to inflict on his sons, either. "Spare the rod and spoil the child" was a fine biblical saying, but his parents had taken it rather seriously when he was a kid. He definitely hadn't been spared.

"I'm sorry, but my mind is made up. Lisa sends some money every month, enough to cover their enrollment."

"That's another thing, son. Accepting anything from Lisa gives her an open doorway to hurt you and the children more in the future. I think you should decline."

Cameron took a deep breath. "I disagree. Lisa had as much to do with their existence as I did. They're her responsibility as much as mine, no matter how she acted."

"But—"

"There isn't a but. Idaho has laws that govern how things work in a divorce."

His mother flinched.

He leaned closer. "Divorce is *not* a bad word, Mom. It's a word that describes the situation in my family. Pretending it didn't happen doesn't help. Do I wish things had been different? Of course, I do. But this is my reality. I don't want to only survive the rest of my life. I want to thrive."

"I'm delighted that you're going to church again, son. It seems like a nice place. Perhaps a bit liberal, but there may not be anything better in this town."

Cameron's patience flew out the window. "Grace Fellowship has made all the difference to me since Lisa left. Pastor Ivan, the men's group, the Sunday school program for the boys, working in the greenhouse garden, everything. They welcomed us with open arms and no judgment." In fact, his parents could learn a lot from his church family.

Dad looked up from the crossword puzzle, eyebrows raised.

Whatever that was about. He didn't want to go so far as to say his parents weren't welcome in his home. He didn't want to say that he and the twins didn't need them in their life. They did. But he needed them to accept his choices and not treat him like a pariah.

Lucky Joanna. Not only was she on her honeymoon — and he could definitely envy that — but with the wedding over, she'd moved out of the basement suite and away from their parents. When she and Grady returned, she'd be living in his fine house clear across town. She wouldn't have to deal with Mom and Dad every single day if she didn't want to. Nope. He had definitely drawn the short straw on this one.

Cameron rose to his feet. "I've taken tomorrow off, so I'll be registering the boys at Grace Greenhouse in the morning. I think they'll really enjoy the program. We spent a lot of hours helping in the gardens there last summer and they had fun. Would you like a cup of tea, Mom?"

"I can get it. You sit down, and let me wait on you."

"I'm perfectly capable. It was just that kind of thinking that caused some of the problems between Lisa and me. I figured the little woman was there to ease my life. Maybe if I had treated her like a partner from the beginning, things would have been different."

"I'm sure I don't know what you're talking about, Cameron. The Bible makes it quite clear women are to take care of their men."

Cameron forced a smile to his lips. "I'm glad it works for you and Dad. But the Bible I've been reading tells me that men and women are equal. That the woman isn't made to serve the man any more than the man is to serve the woman. Both should have the attitude that was in Christ Jesus. You know your Bible, Mom. Doesn't the book of Philippians show that Jesus came to serve us? It's not all about who is greater. It's about loving each other and treating each other with respect."

Mom glanced at Dad, but if his father was listening, he gave no indication.

"Now, what kind of tea would you like? I have black, green, and a few kinds of herbal tea. Some of Joanna's favorites. I'll put the kettle on while you decide."

He drew a deep breath as he entered the kitchen. After filling the kettle, he set it on the stove then leaned both hands against the countertop. *Lord? How can I even think about dating right now with my parents in my life? This is crazy. I can't inflict my parents on Alaina. She'll run screaming, and I won't blame her a bit.*

Last night at the wedding had been all about abandon. Not crazy. Not wild. Just enjoying his sister's reception and meeting a beautiful woman. He hadn't even asked Alaina where she'd been all his life. All he knew was that he'd never seen her before. And yet, she'd been in Grace Fellowship this morning, sitting with Kenia Akers. While he'd dithered, the two of them had disappeared into the June sunshine.

He had her phone number. Too bad he wasn't brave enough to use it.

Chapter 4

THE RENOVATED HOUSE, now a children's center, bustled with activity on registration day. Alaina's assistants Whitney and Cheri had rolled open the patio doors and now roved the fenced-in yard while parents and children explored every nook and cranny. A well-equipped play-ground sat between the covered deck and the greenhouses.

Alaina rotated her shoulders from her spot behind the desk. The summer program would run at full capacity, a testament to how badly the town had needed another full-fledged daycare. Only a few families who'd pre-registered had yet to show up for orientation.

Cameron and his sons crossed in front of the large windows and entered what had been the house's dining room. He'd come. She'd seen the boys' names on the list, and they hadn't been a mirage. She'd see Cameron every day all summer. Maybe spending all that time with the twins would dash some cold reality on her attraction for their father.

"Good morning, Mr. Kraus. Here to register your children?"

"I am." Crinkles appeared at the edges of his eyes as he approached her desk. He was just as good-looking — okay, hot — as he'd seemed Saturday evening. He gripped one twin's hand in each of his.

"I'm Miss Alaina, and I'm the administrator of the Grace summer program. I believe you've pre-registered online." Hopefully, she'd kept her voice even. And smiled at the little boys more than at their father.

"So this is what brought you to Arcadia Valley."

"Yes, it is. I'm well qualified, I assure you. I have a degree in early childhood education and several years of experience working in a daycare in Nampa. I'm thrilled at this opportunity to head up the program here for Grace Fellowship." Somehow, she managed to keep her voice even. This was her job.

"I, for one, am thankful for you." A real smile stretched across his face, seeming to acknowledge there might be a double meaning. "It's been difficult in this town to find adequate care."

"That's what I've heard. I'm thrilled to be here. They say one can never go home again, and it's probably true. Arcadia Valley has grown and changed a lot since I left ten years ago. So, I'm here for a new beginning." Hey, if he could double up meanings on *his* words, so could she.

He dipped his chin, brown eyes twinkling. "Here's to new beginnings."

Alaina could all but see him raising a wine glass in toast,

even though his hands remained on his sons' shoulders. She tore her gaze from his, and looked from one boy to the other before focusing on the redhead. "Your name is Oliver, right?"

The little guy glanced up at his dad then nodded. "Yep. My brother is Evan."

"How old are you and Evan?"

"We're six."

"But we have a birthday soon," Evan interrupted. "Then we'll be seven."

"That's great." Alaina tapped on her tablet and brought up the boys' information. "I see you'll be here Monday through Friday from 8:45 to 5:15." What a long day for them. And for her staff, as the center would be open from seven-thirty to six.

"That's right," Cameron responded. "That's what we get for me having a nine-to-five job."

Alaina nodded. "I get it. We have ten full-time spots for their age group with another twenty flexible spots." And then there was the preschool section. Good thing she had enough trained staff.

She looked up, meeting his eyes once again. She had to stop doing that, because it made the air fizzy and her heart hiccup, which was all kinds of crazy. She'd only just met the guy, after all. And he wasn't her type.

Not that she knew what her type was like. Not after Garth.

"Sign here. Then, if you and the boys would like to have a look around, feel free. We'll be having some structured time and some free time every day. The greenhouse and garden will be part of our curriculum. And we'll have reading and science segments as well."

His eyebrows rose. "Science?"

"Definitely. We'll be studying how things work. We want to encourage curious young minds." She stood, smiling at the boys. "You've probably already read all the information about the summer program. If not, please do have a look around the website. You'll need to send a packed lunch and two snacks for each boy every day. I'm sure we'll supplement from the garden as various vegetables ripen."

Cameron nodded. "I'll refresh myself on the website later today. Where do I add the names of those who can pick up the boys if I'm unable to be here?"

He probably meant his parents. "You can do that online. Just put it in the person's name, his or her phone number… and it would be really helpful if you added a photo."

Behind Cameron, a mom with two little girls peered past his shoulder. Right, Alaina was probably taking too long with him. "Is there anything else I can help you with just now?"

The twinkle in his eyes and the smile that lifted his lips weakened her knees. "Not at the moment. Perhaps later?" His eyebrows lifted.

"You know where to find me."

If anything, his grin got bigger. With a lingering look, Cameron guided his sons away.

Alaina took a deep breath and pulled up a smile as the woman stepped closer. "Good morning. I'm Miss Alaina, and I'm the director for the Grace summer program. And you are…?"

"I'm Dina Poncetta, and these are my daughters, Ophelia

and Isabella. Ophelia just turned seven, and Isabella is four. Both of them are registered for full days Monday, Wednesday, and Friday."

"Pleased to meet you, Ms. Poncetta. And nice to meet you girls, too."

Dina leaned over. "I must say I'm a bit unhappy about having the Kraus twins in the same program. Those two tend to pick on my sweet girls, and their father just lets them go. I depend on you to make sure they behave."

Great. A warning from total strangers was just what she needed.

Cameron was pretty sure he wasn't supposed to have overheard that. Or maybe he was. What was with people in this town, anyway? He was doing the best he could raising the twins. Sure, they were mischievous and a bit rambunctious, but they only needed a little guidance, not to be stomped on by Lisa's former friends. The boys would grow out of it.

Evan tugged on his hand. "Dad, can we go play on the monkey bars?"

"Sure, let's go. Right through those doors."

Oliver giggled. "We know, Dad."

The boys had spent as much time on this property as he had. Cameron had pitched in whenever he could, and he'd been available the day the playground equipment had arrived. How dare Dina Poncetta suggest his sons had any less right to be here than her daughters?

Cameron shook his head. He needed to stop going there. If Alaina were so easily deterred from whatever was budding between them then she wasn't the right woman for him.

Why was he even thinking about a new relationship? If his parents were to be believed, he'd had his one chance at marriage and was now doomed to remain alone for the rest of his life. Was that really how God meant it? No second chances?

The boys ran ahead of him. Evan scrambled up the monkey bars and was soon dangling from his knees. Oliver clambered up a large net that formed one of several ways to reach the lofty slide.

Cameron settled into a chair on the deck. Two young women paced the play area watching the two dozen or so playing children. Evelyn Kujak had spent considerable time interviewing potential staff. Looked like she'd found not only an able administrator in Alaina but several assistants.

A few minutes later Alaina took a seat near him. She didn't look his way, but gazed out across the playground. His pulse sped up as he caught a whiff of her faint perfume. Magnolia, or something floral. Same as she'd worn to the wedding on Saturday, a scent that he'd irrevocably tie to her for the rest of his life.

Was he ready for this? If not now, then when?

He didn't subscribe to the 'never again' theory his parents advocated, did he? No.

He angled toward her. She'd pulled those brown curls into a braid that hung halfway down her back, with tendrils plotting their escape. Long lashes accented her eyes — sparkling brown, he knew, though he couldn't see them clearly at this angle. Her pert nose drew his attention down to pink lips. What would they taste like under his?

She shot a glance in his direction, snagging on his gaze. Her eyes widened slightly. So did her lips.

Cameron should say something. Preferably brilliant. Memorable. "You look great," he said softly.

"Um, thanks." Her gaze darted away then swung back to his.

Awareness all but glittered in the air between them. If he let this opportunity go, he'd regret it forever. Who would ever know what might have been?

"Alaina, would you like to go out this evening? We could go out somewhere for dessert, maybe around eight?" His parents wouldn't mind watching the sleeping boys, would they?

She searched his face, her cheeks pinker than they'd been a few minutes ago. "I'd like that."

"Where do you live? I'll pick you up."

She wrinkled her cute nose. "With my parents until I find a place of my own. Actually, I might be moving in with Kenia Akers soon."

Alaina had chatted with Grady's sister at the wedding reception then again yesterday after church. Why did the thought they might be close friends bother him? Just because Kenia had always seemed stand-offish to Cameron didn't mean she wasn't a decent person.

Out in the playground, Evan dangled upside down on the monkey bars. He wiggled down the rail on his knees, seeming intent on reaching the end. Only when he stretched and caught a blond curl in his fingers did Cameron figure out his goal.

The little girl yelped and smacked his hand away. "Ouch. Don't do that!"

Dina Poncetta hurried across the playground. "Are you okay, Ophelia? Did that boy hurt you?"

That boy? Cameron surged to his feet. "Evan, play nice. No matter how cute you think that little girl is, you shouldn't pull her hair."

Evan pulled himself to sitting on top of the bar and glanced between his dad and Ophelia. Then he made a face, shrugged, and swung down. He ran off to the far corner of the playground where his brother zipped down the slide.

"Sorry about that." Cameron said to Dina. "Boys will be boys."

"That's no excuse." Dina turned and pinned Cameron with a glare. "You need to teach those imps some manners."

It wasn't like he wasn't trying to find the balance with the boys. Not to be a strict disciplinarian as his parents had been, and yet not let them run roughshod over everyone.

Cameron glanced at Alaina, still sitting in the nearby chair. Her lips had tightened and her back was ramrod straight. Was she about to join the group who'd decided he was a lousy father?

Would she even give him a chance? A real one?

Chapter 5

ONEY, YOUR MOTHER and I don't think this is a good idea."

Alaina reached for her purse as she watched out the window for Cameron's car. She didn't even know what he drove. "We're going to the Jukebox, Dad." Of all innocent places. She and her friends had gone hundreds of times in high school.

Dad stood in the doorway to the kitchen, Mom just behind him. "He's a married man. Have you thought about—"

"Divorced."

"Well, yes, but even so—"

"It's not like I'm the one who wrecked his marriage, all right? I didn't even know him then. I've never met his ex."

Mom's hand covered her mouth.

Good grief. It wasn't like Alaina didn't have any misgivings of her own, but she sure couldn't share them with her parents. Was she really considering dating a divorcé? Not considering it. Waiting for him to pull up at the curb.

It hadn't felt so rebellious Saturday night as her parents were making it out to be now. He was just a man she found attractive. A man who happened to have been divorced for several years. A man with two children. The thought of the twins gave her more pause than the fact of his dissolved marriage.

A white sedan stopped along the street. Cameron stepped out of the driver's side and came up the sidewalk, a smile forming as he caught her watching from the window.

Alaina reached for the knob. "See you later." She'd tell them not to wait up for her, but that would likely send the wrong message.

"Let him ring the doorbell and come in for a minute."

"Dad, seriously? I'm twenty-eight. High school is long past."

His eyes narrowed. "Courtesy is still courtesy."

The doorbell buzzed, and Alaina sighed as she opened the door. "Hi, Cameron."

"Hi." The approving smile as he looked her over caused her cheeks to warm. "Ready?"

Dad cleared his throat.

Alaina held back from rolling her eyes, just barely. "Cameron, have you met my parents? Duane and Louise? I believe I told you they own the golf and country club. Mom, Dad, this is Cameron Kraus."

Cameron stretched out his hand. "Pleased to meet you. I've seen you around Grace Fellowship from time to time, haven't I?"

For a second Alaina worried Dad wouldn't accept the greeting, but then his hand reached past her and shook Cameron's. Looked a little extra firm from here, but if Cameron couldn't deal with her father, it was going to be a problem no matter how she sliced it.

"Yes, that's our home church." Mom looked Cameron over.

Alaina edged past him to the stoop. "See you later, Mom and Dad."

Cameron got the hint and followed her out, pulling the door shut behind him.

She stayed a step ahead of him lest he take her hand or something while her parents watched from the living room window. Not that they hadn't seen her in Cameron's arms at the wedding reception.

He opened the car door, and she tucked her skirt around her legs as she settled into the deep bucket seat. A moment later he'd rounded the vehicle and they drove away from the curb.

Cameron grinned at her. "Daddy's girl?"

She blew out a long breath. "You'd think I was fourteen."

He chuckled. "I'm feeling the same way with my parents here for the summer. Joanna's been living in my basement suite since she moved to Arcadia Valley and, with her marriage, it came vacant at the most convenient time for my parents to simply move in. Thankfully, they're returning to England in a couple of months."

"They're watching the twins tonight?"

He nodded, his smile turning to a grimace as he gave a sardonic laugh. "Only after giving me the third degree."

"Oh?"

"I'm divorced, Alaina." His hands tightened on the steering wheel. "I'm sure you figured that out by now and, if not, people will elbow their way over to tell you all about it."

"My parents have reminded me a few times."

Cameron shook his head slightly. "And yet you dare to go out with me? You're brave."

He had no idea. Or maybe he did. "Everyone has a past, Cameron."

"You've been married, too?"

"No. I'm pretty much squeaky clean." Through no fault of Garth's. Maybe that's why he'd had another girlfriend on the side. Or maybe it was Alaina who'd been the spare. Who knew?

"I get that divorce isn't ideal." He shot a glance her way then refocused on the street. "I doubt anyone goes into marriage thinking they'll just end things if it doesn't work out."

"Maybe some do."

"Maybe. I didn't." He bit his lip and turned toward downtown. "I guess I assumed it would be easier than it was. I didn't know Lisa as well as I thought I did. And, well, I was full of myself, I guess. Sure I had enough charisma to carry the day."

He had plenty of it, for sure.

She'd never been on a first date where the man laid out all his shortcomings. Was he purposefully trying to scare her off? Alaina watched him from the corner of her eye as he parallel parked on the street in front of the Jukebox.

This was going to be an interesting evening.

⌒‿‿⌒

Cameron splayed his hand on the small of Alaina's back

as he ushered her into the retro-style café. Her geometric-patterned top lay soft under his palm, and her turquoise skirt swirled above her knees as she walked. Looked like those same strappy sandals from Saturday night, but now her toenails peeked out in vibrant red.

Mom would say that proved she was a hussy.

Mom had a lot of interesting theories.

He wasn't here to think or talk about his parents. There'd been enough heavy stuff in the car on the way over. What had possessed him to talk about his divorce? He'd devote the rest of the evening to getting to know Alaina, not dredging up his past.

"Grab a table!" the waitress called. "Would you like menus?"

"Yes, please." He kept his hand in place, guiding Alaina to a red-padded booth beside a window, where he slid in across from her.

She looked around with a grin. "Wow, this place hasn't changed since I was in high school. This was our favorite hangout."

Cameron grimaced. He should have thought of that. Maybe taken her to L'Aubergine or somewhere that hadn't been open back then. A place not filled with other memories. L'Aubergine was a bit upscale for a first date, though, and the Sunrise wasn't open evenings.

The waitress, clad in a poodle skirt and saddle shoes, slapped two menus on the gray laminate table. "Can I get you coffee?"

"Not for me, thanks," said Alaina. "I'd love a banana split."

Sounded good. Cameron nodded. "Make that two."

"This brings back memories." Alaina's eyes shone as the waitress flounced away. "Thanks for suggesting it."

Maybe this would be all right, after all. "Some of the old restaurants are still around, too. Demi's Delights, the Sunrise, El Corazon... although El Corazon isn't quite as traditionally Mexican as it used to be." He should take her there next time. If there was a next time.

"Javier took it over, didn't he?" Her face brightened. "It's so romantic that he and Molly found each other again after all those years."

From what Cameron had heard, the eldest Quintana sibling had pined for his one lost love for over a decade. Meanwhile Cameron had met Lisa, fallen in love — he had, hadn't he? — married her, fathered twins, and been divorced in half the time. He shook his head. Not going there again tonight.

"Javier and Molly are living in one of those little cottages near El Corazon while they build a new house for themselves and Molly's daughter. They're Kenia's neighbors." Alaina grinned at him. "She's offered I could live with her for a while. They're sure cute places, and my share of the rent would be reasonable. I think they've been built since I left town."

Kenia again. But why shouldn't Alaina have friends in town? Just because he was basically a hermit didn't mean everyone ought to be. But... Kenia? "You know her well?"

Alaina shrugged. "I used to. We hung out in the same crowd in high school, but lost touch when I moved away." She angled a glance up at Cameron. "You probably know her better than I do anymore. Is there something I should know?"

Cameron couldn't put his finger on why he didn't approve of Grady's sister. He shrugged. "I'm sure she's nice enough." Add Kenia to the list of topics not to discuss tonight, if possible. "There's another new restaurant, Fire and Brimstone. Italian-Korean pizza fusion."

She blinked at him, her long lashes sweeping her cheeks. "A what?"

"You knew the Tam family, right? Violet's mom, Shirley, opened it up last summer in that old automotive shop out on First Avenue. She offers some unique combinations." Cameron couldn't help the grin. "Ever had kimchee on pizza before?"

"Can't say that I have." Her lips pulled in, rubbing against each other. "Trying to imagine it."

He tore his gaze away. "You won't have to imagine it for long. How about Friday night?"

Her eyes shot to his again. "Friday?"

Right, their dessert hadn't arrived yet on their first date, and he was planning a second. Maybe a third. He wanted to be the one to show her what Arcadia Valley was like now. He wanted to be by her side. A lot.

The waiter scurried back with two luscious-looking banana splits, piled high with both ice cream and whipped cream then drizzled with chocolate, strawberry, and caramel sauce. A maraschino cherry perched jauntily on the top of each.

"Friday sounds fun." Alaina dipped her spoon into the ice cream, took a bite, then leaned against the padded seat with a happy sigh. "Oh, how I've dreamed of this place since leaving Arcadia Valley. It's even better than I remembered."

Cameron could only hope a little of that might be because of present company, but she'd probably had a string of boyfriends as a teen. She'd hinted at it after her parents had given him the once-over earlier. Or maybe she'd mostly hung out with a group. It didn't much matter now.

"I haven't had a banana split in ages," he confessed. "Probably just as well I haven't introduced the twins to this much sugar in one bowl."

She chuckled and popped the cherry in her mouth, pulling out the stem. "Kids thrive on sugar. I know I did."

He was simply thankful he hadn't had to bring them tonight. Not that he'd ever brought them on a date. He hadn't taken anyone out since Lisa left. He hadn't ever been interested until now. Sure, he'd thought about Evelyn for a while last year, but they'd never got even this far before Ben Kujak came along and swept her off her feet and out of Cameron's sphere.

Watching Alaina's delight in her decadent dessert across from him, Cameron was just as glad. Alaina had been worth waiting for. And, for the first time, it seemed ongoing childcare was solid. He'd already enrolled the boys in the after-school program at Grace once the school year resumed. By then his parents would be gone, but he could find an occasional evening sitter.

His gaze caught on the woman across from him, her brown curls swirling around her heart-shaped face and down the front of her as she licked whipped cream off her spoon. Occasional might not be often enough. *Whoa, Cameron. One day — one date — at a time.*

She glanced over at him. "Did you grow up in England? You don't have a British accent."

Cameron blinked. "Uh, no. We lived a lot of places across the US when Joanna and I were kids. My parents have been in England since I graduated from high school, teaching at a small Bible school. It's the longest they've ever lived in one place."

"Have you been to visit them?"

"A couple of times, early on." When he'd been footloose and fancy-free.

"Did you see Buckingham Palace? The changing of the guard?" She leaned closer, her eyes wide. "Maybe caught a glimpse of Queen Elizabeth?"

He shook his head. "Nope. The school isn't in London but out in the countryside. We didn't do any sightseeing, really."

"That seems a total waste of airfare." Alaina sat back. "If I ever go, you can bet I'll be stalking the places where I might get a glimpse of William and Kate or Harry and Meghan. Or those adorable children. Trust me on that."

He chuckled. Who'd have pegged her for a royal-watcher? "The English countryside is beautiful. All green and lush, with history everywhere. Far more interesting than princes and princesses."

"So you say." Her lips turned up and her eyes gleamed.

He leaned on the table. "Although the Bible school *is* housed in an old castle. There's even a set of Roman-era ruins out beyond the stables."

"Now you're talking."

Their eyes aligned for a long moment. Was she thinking

what he was thinking? That maybe, someday, they'd go together?

It was much too soon to be thinking long term. But he wasn't built to flirt his way from one woman to the next like a hummingbird sampling nectar from many flowers. No, he was built to stay the course. It was Lisa who'd left. Not him.

Chapter 6

"OPHELIA IS JUST FINE, Dina. She can hold her own."
The child leaned against her mother, sniffling.
Dina narrowed her gaze at Alaina. "She shouldn't
have to hold her own. I trusted the staff here to make sure all
the children treat each other with respect."

Like Alaina had eyes on the back of her head. No daycare
could afford a one-on-one ratio, though sometimes it seemed
that was required where the Kraus boys were concerned. It
had been an exhausting week. "We're doing our best."

"That twin dumped sand in my daughter's hair." She
pointed at the blond watching at the window for his dad to
arrive.

That twin was Evan, and he wasn't the only one awaiting
Cameron's arrival. Alaina would prefer Dina to be long gone
by then. "I'll make sure the staff knows to watch more
closely."

"Please do." Dina wrapped an arm around her daughter.
"Where's Isabella? It's time to go."

"With Cheri in the preschool area." Alaina gave her a

smile. "See you Monday. Have a great weekend!"

She was certainly looking forward to hers, starting with a second date with Cameron this evening. She hadn't spoken to him all week other than during drop-off and pick-up, which had been all about the boys. Unless texting counted, as there had been some of that as well... not about the boys.

Dina and Ophelia headed for the space reserved for the younger children just as Evan yelped, "Dad!"

Alaina's heart skipped a beat. Just as it had done every time she'd seen Cameron all week. She should probably be busy somewhere else, except that she was the staff member in charge of signing children out today. In fact, she'd made it her responsibility every night this week. She was in charge. That made it her job, right?

"Hi, guys."

The twins launch themselves at their father, and he swept them both up into his strong arms with a laugh. His brown eyes grew even warmer when he looked past their heads and caught her watching. "Good afternoon, Miss Alaina. I hope Oliver and Evan were good kids today."

It was all Alaina could do not to shift her gaze to the preschool room where Dina had just disappeared, but her relief was short-lived.

"Those boys are nothing but little hoodlums," came Dina's irate voice. "If someone were teaching them better manners at home, they might be an asset to a daycare like this one."

Uh oh.

Cameron's gaze narrowed as he turned to see Dina coming into the main area carrying Isabella and holding

Ophelia by the hand. "What did they do now?"

Wasn't it better if the parents talked about it themselves? But she was still the person in charge. Interfere? Not interfere? While she was trying to decide, Dina marched closer to Cameron.

"They do nothing but pick on my daughter."

That wasn't entirely fair. All the children had done a whole lot of things today before the sand bath had occurred.

"I'm sorry to hear it." Cameron's voice stayed even as he looked from one twin to the other, who were still in his arms. "What did you do, boys?"

Oliver pushed his brother in the chest. "Not me. Him."

"Nothing much." Evan scowled.

"Evan."

The blond twin sighed. "It was just sand. That's all."

Cameron glanced at Dina, and so did Alaina. Ophelia's mother did not look mollified. "Did you say you were sorry, son?"

Evan's small shoulder lifted in a shrug. "Sorry," he mumbled.

"There you go." Cameron's eyebrows rose as he look at Dina. "Is that what you wanted?"

"I don't think it was sincere."

Alaina chomped on her lip. The kid was not quite seven, for crying out loud. Dina was expecting a miracle.

"It's the best we can do at the moment." Cameron slid both twins to the floor. "You boys go get your backpacks, okay?"

Dina's gaze narrowed as she and her daughters swept past the trio in the doorway. The door clicked shut behind her as the boys scampered away.

Alaina took a step closer, her gaze fixed on Cameron's. What did the other woman have against him anyway? "Sorry about that."

He shrugged. "Some people seem to think that kids should be born with good manners. I'm here to tell you they're not. And, besides, boys are rougher than girls."

She felt her brows rise. "We don't treat girls and boys any differently here. All the children are expected to learn respect and manners."

"Isn't that what I just said?"

Not exactly.

The boys dashed back into the room slinging their packs over thin shoulders. "We're ready, Dad. Let's go!"

"We still good for tonight?" Cameron's dark eyes were unreadable.

"Absolutely. What time?"

"My parents are taking the boys to the drive-through in Twin Falls in a bit." He glanced at the clock on the wall. "It's almost five-thirty now. How about six-thirty?"

Alaina sank into the depths of his eyes. "Sounds good. How about if I meet you there?"

"But it's a date. I want to pick you up."

She didn't want her parents to grill him again. Not that they really had on Monday, but they certainly put her through the questioning when she returned. It probably didn't matter. She was going to get it afterward, regardless. It wasn't as though she were going to lie about where she was going and who she'd be with. "Okay."

"Everything all right?"

"Dad," whined Evan, tugging at his arm.

Alaina pushed out a smile. "Sounds like you need to go. I'll see you soon."

His gaze softened slightly, and she felt as though he caressed her with his eyes. Then he nodded, turned, and nudged his boys out the door ahead of him.

"Whoa. What's going on around here? Did I miss something?" asked Cheri from behind her.

Alaina turned to see a grin on her coworker's face. "Not really."

Cheri poked her chin toward the parking lot. "You've got a hot date tonight with someone's daddy?"

A date, anyway. And it was difficult to forget, even for a minute, that he was a father.

The atmosphere at Fire and Brimstone was loud and jovial. Cameron preferred a more subdued scene, but watching the light in Alaina's eyes as she looked around the renovated automotive garage was worth it.

Alaina looked up at him. "This is so cool!"

"Arcadia Valley's newest sensation," he said. "This town isn't hurting for great places to eat." There were sure more options — better options — than there'd been when he moved to town eight years back.

"Look, there's Violet! Did you say you know her?" Alaina waved at a young woman with long black hair.

The woman set down a large pizza at a table near the

sliding doors through which cars had once been driven. She rushed over and enveloped Alaina in a hug. "Alaina Silva! It's been years since I've seen you. What are you up to?"

"I just moved back to Arcadia Valley a couple of weeks ago." Alaina hugged the girl back. "I'm the administrator for the new preschool and day care program at Grace Fellowship. We just got started this past week. How about you?"

"I teach over at the elementary school." Violet glanced at Cameron.

"That's great. I'd like you to meet my... friend, Cameron. We've just recently met."

A twinkle formed in Violet's eyes. "That's great." She leaned closer and whispered, "Did you hear I married Silas Black?"

Alaina's eyes widened. "No way. You have got to be kidding me."

"It's really true. I can't even tell you how much he has changed since high school."

Cameron had no idea what was going on. He let his hand rub Alaina's back gently. Maybe that would remind her that she was here on a date, not on a gabfest with her old friends.

"You'll have to tell me all about it one of these days. Meanwhile, it looks like you have a full house here. Are there any open tables?"

Good. She'd got the hint.

"I think Nico and Charlotte are just leaving. Let me check with them."

Cameron pulled Alaina a little closer as Violet hurried over to talk to a small family. "Or we could just get something to go."

"We can do that if you want. But it would be kind of fun to watch them make our pizza right here." She pointed as the waist-height open hearth in the kitchen beyond. "This is amazing."

Loud music rocked the place, and Cameron sighed. Not that they would be able to hear each other. The couple with the small girl rose to their feet and followed Violet over to the cash register. Violet waved at Alaina and Cameron. "Grab the table!" she called. "I'll get someone to wipe up in just a minute."

They were stuck here, then. What this place lacked in atmosphere compared to L'Aubergine, it certainly made up for in vibe. Why hadn't he ever noticed how loud it was before? Probably because he hadn't been on a date. With any luck, they could eat quickly and head out somewhere else. Maybe for a walk along Arcadia Creek. He wanted to know all about her, and that discussion seemed unlikely here.

Should've thought about the atmosphere sooner, Kraus.

He seated her on an industrial chair at the metal table just as a young server gathered the plates and glasses. She came back just seconds later, wiped the table, and presented them with menus. "Would you like to start with drinks?"

"Sure. I'd like a cola. What would you like, Alaina?"

Alaina looked from him to the menu to the server. "I'd like iced tea if you have any."

"No problem." The girl hurried away.

Alaina watched her friend Violet as the other woman bustled in and out of the open kitchen. It was like she'd rather talk to her friend than to him.

Cameron reached across both closed menus and captured

Alaina's hands. "Have you had a chance to decide what you'd like to order?"

Her gaze snapped back to his, and her cheeks pinked. "No, I'm sorry. What have you tried here that you like?"

Before he could answer, Violet stood beside their table setting down their drinks. "We have a special tonight on the Korean beef and sprouts pizza. Can I interest you in that one?"

Alaina's eyebrows raised as she looked at Cameron. "That sounds interesting. What do you think? Did you have something else in mind?"

Cameron shrugged. "Sure. We can give it a try." Weren't his parents taking the twins to Pizza Hut tonight? It almost sounded better, other than the company. Well, it had been his idea to come to Fire and Brimstone with Alaina. Just because he had momentarily forgot that she once knew everyone in town didn't mean that this was a bad place to bring her.

Violet tapped the order into her tablet and scurried off to the kitchen.

Finally. He toyed with Alaina's fingers on the tabletop. "How was your week?"

"Busy. It seems weird being back in my hometown after all these years." She shook her head.

The music pounded around them, but somehow it faded into the background. "Thanks for coming with me tonight," he said softly. "I was going to ask you if you'd like to come to Craters of the Moon National Monument with us tomorrow. The boys have been begging. And then I remembered that my parents are here, and that my car seats five." He gave her a rueful grin. "Maybe another time."

"I'm busy tomorrow, anyway. Did I tell you I'm moving in with Kenia? She's renting one of those cute Valley Cottages over near El Corazon. It will be great to get out of my parents' house again. Three weeks has been long enough."

That would make it easier for her. All he had to think was how much he'd hate to live with his parents again to realize how much the situation had chafed her. But with Kenia? "I'm happy for you." Mostly.

"You seem to have something against Kenia." Her eyebrows rose as though challenging him to deny it, and her hands pulled away.

"Not really. I don't know her well enough to have an opinion." And he didn't want to, for all that she was his sister's sister-in-law.

"She's really nice. I mean, we lost touch when I went away to college. She left, too. She went off to University of Utah and I went to Boise U. I never thought I'd see her back in Arcadia Valley running a bookstore, of all things."

"I know her parents wanted her to take over the flower shop, but she has too many allergies."

"Well, that explains a few things."

He didn't really want to talk about Kenia anymore. He hadn't wanted to talk about her in the first place. Or Violet. Or anyone, really. Alaina was way more extroverted than he was. Could he do this? Was she worth it? He filled his gaze with her pretty pink top that brought out the glow in her cheeks. Her brown eyes peeked up at him through lowered lashes. She was beautiful. She was genuinely nice. She went to his church. He could do a lot worse. In fact, he already had.

Cameron had a sip of his cola. "Tell me what makes Alaina Silva tick."

It better not be shopping and having coffee with her friends. Because that would be way too much like Lisa all over again.

Chapter 7

OM PURSED HER LIPS as she looked around the tiny cottage. "Alaina, I don't understand why you're doing this. Our basement is so much bigger than the space you will share here."

Alaina choked back a sigh. "I left home ten years ago, Mom. Women my age don't move back in with their parents. It was fine to stay for a couple of weeks until I found my own place — and thank you for the offer — but you couldn't really have expected me to stay indefinitely."

By the look on Mom's face, yes, she could've.

Alaina slung her arm over her mother's shoulder. "Be glad I'm in the same town again, okay? I'm gainfully employed, I'll soon have my first paycheck, and being on my own again is good."

"You're not on your own."

Trust Mom to state the obvious. "I had roommates most of the time in Nampa, too. You knew that, and it never bothered you." Alaina hesitated. "What's different this time?" She wasn't sure she wanted to know, come to think of it.

Mom glanced around the space and shook her head.

"Say what's on your mind, Mom. Kenia's popped over to borrow some eggs from Veronica Quintana, so no one will overhear."

"She's sometimes a bit wild, you know."

"Kenia?"

Mom nodded. "I don't know if there's any truth to the rumor."

Her friend was full of fun, but Alaina hadn't seen anything — yet — that made her wary. "She has a good heart. She teaches Sunday school, and she manages a bookstore. I think I need to know more about this speculation before I take it too seriously." Although, hadn't Cameron seemed uneasy, too?

"Don't say I didn't warn you."

"Just because we share this little house doesn't mean we'll do everything together. We have quite different jobs, and I'll be out with—" She snapped her mouth shut.

"A divorced man."

"We've been over this. You haven't convinced me that divorce is the big unforgivable sin. Aren't there ever extenuating circumstances? It's Lisa who left Cameron, not the other way around."

"She wouldn't have if he'd treated her right."

Seriously? Alaina drew her eyebrows up. "He's a total

gentleman. I can tell you Cameron opened more doors for me this week than Garth did all last year." She eyed her mother. "And don't be getting any ideas about how much time we've spent together. That was over two dates, both of which you knew about."

"You can't make us like the situation. We've heard things—"

"It sounds like you are listening to way too much gossip. You need to trust my judgment, Mom. Pray for me, definitely. Give advice when I ask for it, but please give me real reasons and not hearsay."

"Your father and I just want what's best for our girls. You can't fault us for that."

They'd been in Adriana's business just last Christmas, and Adriana was six years older than Alaina with two kids. Maybe it was futile to think anything could change. On the other hand, Adriana lived in Spokane and didn't have to deal with their parents every day. She and her new husband would be visiting Arcadia Valley for the Fourth of July, and Alaina couldn't wait for some girl time. She'd been used to calling Adriana whenever she needed someone to talk to, but it didn't seem right to keep up that habit now that her sister was remarried. She couldn't expect Myles to understand their bond.

"Not faulting you, Mom. Just asking you to trust the job you've already done raising me. In the ten years since I left home the first time, I haven't killed anyone, stolen anything, or slept around. You and Dad must have done something right, don't you think?"

Mom's hand swept the small cottage. "There are other

places to rent in this town. Bigger. Nicer."

"Not as many options as you'd think. The lease is in Kenia's name, and she's well able to pay it without me. If something else comes up, I'll let her know and move on. I think you're worrying over nothing." The big question was, were her parents more concerned about Kenia or about Cameron? Or were neither of Alaina's relationships the real worry, and they were simply being the overbearing parents they'd always been? Mom cried wolf so often, Alaina had no idea how to tell if the caution was called for this time or not.

From outside, Kenia's cheerful voice called out to a neighbor.

"Or your father and I can help you with the down payment to buy a house." Mom looked at Alaina expectantly.

"Sometime I would love to own my own place, but I'll save up for it myself." Alaina could only imagine how tied to her parents she'd feel if she accepted that much money from them. Besides, who knew if she'd be able to hack living in Arcadia Valley long-term? If things worked out with Cameron, sure. If they didn't, the town might feel too small, especially since she saw his children every day.

Alaina reeled slightly at the thought of that kind of permanence. She'd only known Cameron for a week. Dancing at the wedding and two dates since then. He was actually moving pretty fast, but it didn't feel like it.

"Good afternoon, Mrs. Silva." Kenia breezed through the door.

"Hello, Kenia." Mom glanced around one more time. "Well, I should be going. Will you come for dinner tonight, Alaina?"

Her mother was sure trying hard. "Not tonight. I just moved out." Alaina forced a laugh. "You can't possibly miss me yet."

"I missed you every minute that you lived in Nampa." Mom sighed, cast a glance toward Kenia once again, then swept out the door.

A moment later the car engine began to purr.

Kenia turned to Alaina. "What was that all about?"

Alaina shook her head. "I have no idea. My mother seems to think you have some sort of reputation in this town."

Kenia's lips tightened. "Right."

Cameron stood in the foyer at Grace Fellowship after church the next morning, waiting for Oliver and Evan to dash in from Sunday school. Thankfully, Grady's parents, Barry and Linda Akers, had drawn his mom and dad off to the side and were chatting with them. Joanna and Grady would be back from their honeymoon in a few days, and it seemed both sets of their parents were finally taking some time to get to know each other after the bustle of the wedding.

Alaina and Kenia exited the sanctuary from the far set of doors. He hadn't seen Alaina since Friday night, the longest he'd gone since meeting her a week before. There was no way his heart should be thumping this wildly at the sight of her in such a short time. How could he trust himself? He'd fallen for Lisa, fast and hard, back in the day, and look how that had turned out. Oh, Alaina was different. He was different now. Lisa had only come to church with him a few times a year, and only when he begged her. After a couple of years, he hadn't bothered. Either with the begging, or with the going himself.

Lord, I'm sorry. I'm sorry I let someone else pull me away from my relationship with You.

Alaina wouldn't do that, would she? She was a believer in her own right. She laughed at something Kenia had said, and then her eyes caught on his. His mouth went dry as though swabbed with cotton balls. All he could do was stare. She wore a white lacy top today, paired with a pale green skirt. He had to admit her knee-length skirts gave a flirty vibe while being completely modest. But it was her face he couldn't take his eyes off, framed in those long brown curls. When could he kiss her?

Oh, Kraus, you're in deep trouble.

"Good morning, Alaina." He closed the gap between them, ignoring Kenia at her side. "You look beautiful today."

She angled her head to one side and gave him a once-over. A grin played with her lips and danced in her eyes. "You look pretty good yourself."

Kenia looked between them then bumped Alaina's arm. "I'll see you back at the cottage later. I need to talk to Ursula for a minute."

Just when Cameron thought he might have a chance to talk to Alaina without interruption, Evelyn and Ben came out of the sanctuary, hand in hand. Evelyn gave Alaina a hug. "We were just talking about you. Would you like to come out to the house for lunch?"

Alaina glanced at Cameron. Was this his cue to say they already had plans? But they didn't, really. He'd be happy to come up with something on the fly, just to spend time with her.

The twins clattered in with Maisie between them. "Can we go to Maisie's house and ride Rapunzel, Dad?"

Ben looked between Cameron and Alaina then over at the children and back to Cameron, his eyes twinkling. "Now that sounds like a good idea, don't you think, love?" He leaned against Evelyn.

Cameron glanced over to where his parents were still talking with Barry and Linda. "I'm not sure what my parents' plans are." But they had spent all day yesterday together out at the National Monument. It wasn't like they'd agreed to have every meal together while they lived in Arcadia Valley. The lower suite had its own kitchen. "Let me just tell them we have other plans for lunch." He looked at Evelyn. "If you're sure."

Evelyn laughed. "We'd love to have you all. Maisie has been begging for the twins to come over for a while now. If today is the day, that's great."

Cameron excused himself and crossed the foyer.

Mom turned when he touched her elbow. "I was just coming to find you, son. Barry and Linda have invited us for lunch at the Sunrise."

Sweet relief. "Then you won't mind if the boys and I go out to Ben and Evelyn's for the afternoon."

Mom shot a quick glance at Linda Akers. "You're more than welcome to join us."

"Oh, no, that's all right. I'll see you back at the house later." He made good his escape.

"That worked out rather well," he said to Evelyn a moment later. "They've got other plans."

"That's settled then." Evelyn turned to Alaina. "Have you been out to the acreage yet? Do you know how to find us?"

"She can ride with me and the boys," Cameron offered.

Oliver pulled at his arm. "Are we going to Maisie's house?"

"We are." Cameron turned to Evelyn. "Is there something I can bring?"

She waved a hand. "I think we've got plenty. Just bring yourselves."

Ben slid his arm around Evelyn's waist and tugged her closer to his side. Just last summer that sight had caused mild jealousy to flare in Cameron. Even a few months ago, he'd felt wistful about Evelyn. For some reason, his mind had latched onto her as a possible wife. Now he knew he'd never loved her. She'd been right to insist on only being friends, even though it hurt at the time. Had he only wanted to protect her? She and Maisie had been through so much, but so had Ben. His friends were perfect for each other.

Was Alaina just right for him? Was he really falling in love, or just looking for a companion and someone to help with the twins? No, not with Alaina. She stirred something in him he hadn't felt in a long time.

Chapter 8

LAINA SAT ON EVELYN and Ben's back deck with a glass of iced tea in her hand. Not far away, Maisie led Rapunzel around the corral with Oliver on the pony's back, while Evan perched on the wide plank fence, watching. Arcadia Creek tumbled in the distance, a soothing sound. A gentle breeze stirred the leaves in the large willow tree nearby, bringing with it the fragrance from Evelyn's flowerbeds at the base of the deck.

This was the life. And the best thing in it was Cameron sitting on a deck chair beside her, laughing at something Ben had said. Could this be some kind of reality? She could get used to hearing the rich, deep timbre of his laugh. Why hadn't she noticed when Garth stopped laughing with her? That they no longer had fun together? That they'd grown apart? She'd been crushed at Nikki's evidence at the time. Now she only felt relief.

Evelyn lowered herself into the swing near Alaina. "So how's it going, settling back into Arcadia Valley after so many years away?"

Man, that was a loaded question. It wasn't anything like

what she had dreamed of. She'd never expected to be swept off her feet by a handsome man within days of arrival. She angled a glance at Evelyn. "It's gone amazingly well, actually. I'd forgotten how much I love it here." She chuckled. "It's definitely going to help living with Kenia instead of my parents, though."

"I can just imagine." Evelyn laughed. She glanced around to where Cameron and Ben strolled toward the corral with Ben's dog, Gypsy, at their heels. "So... is there anything going on that I should know about?"

"I think that's the million-dollar question." Alaina couldn't help the grin that swept across her face. "I know it's much too soon to really know anything at all but, as you may have noticed, Cameron and I have kind of hit it off."

"I'm really happy for him if that's the case. He's a terrific guy. You should probably know he asked me out a few times last year." Evelyn lifted one shoulder in a slight shrug. "I've always liked him, but not that way, if you know what I mean."

Alaina nodded. "I do know what you mean." She watched the two men flank Evan as they leaned on the fence. The little guy looked up at his dad and said something she couldn't hear. Cameron ruffled the boy's hair.

Ben turned toward the house. "Hey, do you girls want to come down to the creek? The kids need a dunking to cool off."

Evelyn glanced at Alaina. "Do you want to?"

Alaina rose to her feet. "I'd love to see more of your property. I think we're really close to the swimming hole we used to come to all the time when we were kids."

Evelyn chuckled. "Yes, it's less than a quarter mile down the creek. We drove right past it on our way from town."

"I thought the road looked familiar. I guess I didn't bother to remember, since I never thought I'd be living here again."

Cameron turned and leaned back against the railing beside his son. His eyes stayed focused on Alaina.

"He's got it bad." Evelyn stretched and ambled down the steps into the yard. "Are you coming?" she tossed over her shoulder.

Ben lifted Oliver off Rapunzel's back and gave the pony a pat, sending her into the shade where the flick of the other horses' tails kept the flies off of her. Maisie and the twins bounded down the trail toward the creek.

"I'll go with them." Evelyn broke into a jog. "We trust Maisie down there by herself now, but I'm not sure anyone should trust those twins farther than they can throw them."

Cameron chuckled. "I'm sure they'll be fine if you're keeping an eye on them."

Ben grasped Evelyn's hand and hurried down the trail with her, leaving Alaina and Cameron staring at each other. He held out his hand. A magnet pulled her toward him. What harm could holding hands do? She tangled her fingers with his, thrilled with the warmth they evoked.

He gave her fingers a little squeeze as they wandered down the trail, his sleeve fluttering against her bare shoulder. "Do you know Evelyn well?"

Alaina shook her head. "She's the person who interviewed me via Skype a couple of months ago. I guess technically Grace Fellowship is my boss, but Evelyn is their face and their voice. She's gone out of her way to make sure I have everything I need to run the programming effectively."

"She's a good person to have in charge," Cameron said. "She's very thorough. I know it took her months of work to get through all the red tape setting up the program required."

Alaina shuddered. "That sounds like a nightmare to me."

Cameron's fingers tightened around hers as he chuckled. "I get to do a lot of that kind of detail on the day job, myself."

"You work for Stargil, right? I don't even know what you do there."

"Working my way up to a corner office," he said lightly.

What was that supposed to mean? She didn't even know. She raised her eyebrows as she looked up at him.

He bumped her arm, his brown eyes simmering. "It mostly means that I'm trying to make myself as indispensable as possible."

"What department do you work in?" For some reason, she had assumed he worked in the potato chip plant. But a line worker wouldn't have an office at all, let alone a corner one.

"I'm a number cruncher."

"Like... you work in bookkeeping?"

He nodded. "I'm an accountant, actually."

Was this where she said that seemed like an interesting job? She didn't think she could make that sound believable. Of all things, working with numbers was just about her biggest nightmare. "My sister, Adriana, is a bookkeeper for several small businesses in Spokane."

Cameron grinned. "I'm not hearing you profess a deep fascination for ledgers."

"And you'd be right. I can't even stand Sudoku."

"You're kidding me, right? Those puzzles are the best brain-sharpeners in existence."

"Uh, no. That would be books. Stories."

They wandered around the last bend in the trail and nearly ran into Evelyn and Ben sitting on a rock, watching the children play in the creek. If Cameron was worried that his kids were soaking wet, he didn't seem to show it. Mind you, they weren't wearing tuxedos today. She stifled a giggle.

Evelyn turned, glancing from Alaina to Cameron. "What's so funny?" she asked with a knowing grin. "Or dare I ask?"

Alaina cast her mind back. "Cameron just told me he's an accountant. I'm trying to decide if I should run for the hills this afternoon or wait until the cover of darkness."

Ben chuckled. His eyes slid over their joined hands, and his eyes twinkled. "I'd say if running is your plan, you should get on it as soon as possible."

Alaina tipped her head up. Cameron's laughing eyes looked back at her. Wow, she'd missed this. Missed having someone special in her life. Someone who could tease her. Someone that made her think that crunching numbers might even be a good thing, so long as she didn't have to perform the task herself. On the other hand... she pulled herself free of Cameron's grasp, turned, and darted up the path.

Evelyn's and Ben's laughter joined forces as she ran. Oh, man, this was crazy. Why was she making a big deal of his choice of career? Would Cameron think she was serious? Maybe she was. Maybe all this time she had no idea what she was doing, and the flutters in her stomach made her wonder if things weren't moving rather quickly.

But then she heard his footsteps behind her, closing in. Should she play hard to get?

∽ℓᶜ

Cameron caught Alaina around the waist with both hands as she lunged toward the back steps of Ben and Evelyn's house. "Run from me, will you?" he growled, trying to sound as threatening as he could between gales of laughter.

She stilled immediately, and he rammed right into her, knocking her to the grass and landing on her back. He scrambled off her and rolled to sitting beside her head. "Are you okay, Alaina? I'm sorry I tripped over you." Man, he was bungling this. He was treating her as though she were one of the twins, whom he could just scoop up in his arms and carry off, kicking and screaming. That was not what today's well-bred young woman was looking for in husband material. The smile froze on his face as she turned onto her side. She propped her head up on her fist and looked at him in a way she never had before. What was going through her mind? "Did I hurt you?"

She shook her head slowly, her eyes never leaving his. "I'm okay. I don't know why I ran away from you. It was just a joke."

"It's okay." He reached over and brushed her tousled curls from her face.

Her breath drew in sharply. "Evelyn probably thinks I'm crazy. She probably wonders if I'm sane enough to run the daycare and preschool anymore."

"I'm pretty sure she's smarter than that."

"You think so?"

"Nobody has ever told me they were this terrified of numbers before."

A small smile played at the edges of her mouth. "But this is the first time you met *me*."

She hadn't moved away from his touch. In fact, if anything, she leaned slightly into his hand. He slid his fingers the length of her jaw, rubbing her cheekbone gently with his thumb. "You're right. I never did meet you before now. And yet, in this past week, it feels like I've known you forever."

She pushed away from him then, sitting straight up on the grass, her legs curled to one side.

He could only hope there weren't grass stains on that pretty skirt of hers. He might know numbers, but getting stains out was something else. Although Joanna had taught him quite a bit in the year and a half since she'd moved to Arcadia Valley to help him with the twins. She'd worked some magic on their laundry.

Cameron stared into Alaina's eyes. Why was he thinking about laundry? Why, when there was a beautiful woman right in front of him, who didn't seem to be immune to his charms? Who knew he even had charms? He could feel a wry grin taking over his face. "Alaina?"

She looked down to where her hand plucked tufts of green grass and tossed them aside.

She wasn't thinking of tossing him aside in the same way, was she? No, not with the way she'd pressed against his touch a moment ago. "Alaina, may I kiss you? I know we haven't known each other for long, but I'd really like to."

Her head remained dipped down, but she peeked at him through her lowered lashes. His thumb brushed against the soft tips of them.

Alaina nodded slightly and Cameron's heart leaped in his chest. This was such an awkward angle from where they'd been sprawled on the ground. He got to his knees and reached both hands toward her. She took his hands, matching his position, and leaned closer, her eyelids fluttering closed.

Cameron stretched the few inches separating them.

"Dad! Daddy! Where are you?"

Alaina's eyes sprang open.

Cameron surged to his feet, pulling her up with him. "Later," he whispered, turning toward the path just as the boys tore around the corner, Maisie hot on their heels. Evan skidded to a stop in front of Cameron, dripping wet. "Where did you go, Dad? Ben said we could maybe go fishing sometime. He said there's trout in the creek. Can we go fishing?"

Cameron felt chilled, as though a cloud had come between him and the sun. His fingers reached for Alaina's but didn't find them. "I'm sure we can do that sometime, son." He turned to Alaina, who stood with both arms wrapped around her middle a few feet away. "Do you like fishing?"

Her eyes bounced from him to the twins to Maisie and back again. "I've never gone fishing."

Between fishing and Sudoku, there might be some things he could teach her. No doubt there were many things she could teach him... if his two little hoodlums didn't completely scare her away first.

Chapter 9

"A LAINA! COME QUICKLY!" Cheri's voice called urgently.

Alaina surged from her desk, not bothering to glance out the window before dashing toward the patio doors that opened onto the deck. Wailing met her ears. "Ophelia? What happened, honey?" She leaned over the little girl, crumpled on the grass near the climbing mesh. "Did you fall off the ropes?"

"Evan pushed me."

Alaina closed her eyes for a brief second. That boy never seemed to give Ophelia a break. "Are you hurt?" All she needed was a child with broken bones to get negative attention, not only from Dina Poncetta, but also from Grace Fellowship and the Idaho licensing board. Especially in only the second week they were open.

The little girl moaned.

"Where are you hurt?" Alaina brushed the girl's back. "Can you wiggle your toes? How about your fingers?"

Ophelia pushed herself to sitting, then scowled as she crossed her arms in front of her. "I don't want to go to summer school with Evan Kraus. And his brother is stupid, too."

Further away, Alaina could hear Cheri talking to the twins. At least someone was handling the little rascals. Better Cheri than her. "I'm sorry you feel that way, honey." She was even more sorry at how relentless Evan was. And the fact that she might have to talk to his father about his behavior in the program. Oh, she wanted to talk to Cameron all right. Just not about his sons misbehaving. There wasn't much romance in that.

"Why do you think Evan does that to you all the time?"

Ophelia shrugged as she dashed the back of her hand across her face, wiping up the last of her tears.

"Is it that you want to play with him and Oliver, but he doesn't want you to?"

The little girl's face drew into a scowl. "He's dumb. I don't want to play with him. I want him to go away."

"I can't make him do that." Well, it probably was within her jurisdiction to remove the child from the program if things got much worse, but it wasn't a power she wanted to use. Not on Evan, not on Ophelia, not on anyone. Why couldn't they all just get along?

"I'm going to tell my mommy."

Ophelia had probably tattled on Evan every single day since last week Monday. Thankfully the Poncetta girls were only here three days a week. But still, Evan ricocheted from one escapade to another, barely gasping for breath in between.

"Miss Cheri is talking to Evan right now. May be he will be nicer after this." One could hope.

The look Ophelia gave her showed that she didn't share the faint hope.

Alaina sighed. How could she keep the peace? "I promise that if Evan doesn't start behaving, I will talk to his dad about it."

Ophelia bounced to her feet. "Promise?"

Had the little girl made up everything just to get Evan in trouble and to extract this pledge from Alaina? Surely her seven-year-old brain wasn't capable of that, although it might be. Her mother definitely was. Would she put her daughter up to this? The alternative was Ophelia making it up completely, which wasn't likely. Alaina really did need to talk to Cameron about his son.

A scuffle off to the side drew her attention to Cheri's approach as she held Evan's hand in hers. The little boy kicked a clump of grass with nearly every step.

"What do you say?" came Cheri's soft voice. She really was good with the kids.

Evan scowled and muttered, "Sorry."

"Speak up, buddy. We can't hear you. Plus we need a full sentence of what you're sorry about."

"Sorry for pushing you, Ophelia." The singsong style of his voice made a mockery of the correct words.

Alaina met Cheri's glance. What could they do about it? She looked at Ophelia.

The little girl's chin was raised and her eyes glittering as she stared at Evan. "Fine."

Alaina let out a long slow breath. It seemed these two

kids deserved each other, although she doubted Dina would agree. She pointed toward the greenhouse. "Anyone want to come help me pick some lettuce? You can take it home for your sandwiches if you want. Or maybe your mom or dad can use it to make a salad."

Oliver tucked his hand into hers. "I'll come, Miss Alaina."

"How about you, Evan? Do you boys like lettuce?"

Evan made a show of sticking his finger in his mouth and gagging. "Lettuce is yucky." But he turned toward the greenhouse with her, anyway.

"My brother doesn't like vegetables."

Alaina looked down at Oliver. "How about you?"

He shrugged, as she pushed open the greenhouse door. Warm, moist air nearly suffocated her. She probably needed to open the vents further. Operating a greenhouse at the correct temperatures was not something she had learned in her early childhood education classes. Come to think of it, it wasn't something she had learned anywhere at all.

She and the boys wandered down the gravel aisle between two rows of potting tables. Whitney and a small group of preschoolers were busily transplanting sunflowers into larger pots. The seedlings would be lucky to survive the attention.

"So, Evan, what's the problem between you and Ophelia? It seems that you two cause a ruckus more often than any other kids in the program."

The little boy lifted and dropped his shoulder in a way Alaina was becoming far too used to.

"What do you think, Oliver?"

Evan scowled at his twin.

"She won't leave him alone," supplied Oliver.

Much as Alaina had expected to hear. But how could she keep the peace?

Cameron added a few scraps of lettuce to each of their plates. It wasn't like he'd planned to have salad tonight, but the boys had brought it home. Mom's eyebrows rose as she looked between him and the table. Whatever. It was his night for dinner. She shouldn't complain at the takeout burgers and fries. A slice of tomato and a bit of wilted lettuce inside each sesame-seed bun were all the veggies he had planned. She ought to be glad there was a bonus leaf.

"Son, don't you think it's time you learned to cook?"

"It's after five-thirty before I get home with the boys. Monday to Friday. Every week. We don't have burgers all the time."

"No, the other night it was pizza. And the night before that it was tacos."

Cameron leveled a stare at his mother. "I'm sorry you don't seem to think I am taking care of my children the way you want me to. Joanna did a lot of the cooking when she lived downstairs. It really helped." Did he truly want his mother to take over while they were in Arcadia Valley? Well, yes, if it meant she'd quit nagging at him, and he didn't have to deal with meals.

"Maybe I can teach you some quick and easy meals to put together."

"Like you taught *Joanna* when she was a teenager?" He hadn't meant the words to sound so bitter, but he couldn't help it. In his parents' world, cooking was a woman's job. That meant the main option open to him had consisted of finding a wife who could fix meals. Ironically, Lisa had been a lousy cook, but she'd been gone for several years, leaving Cameron to muddle through on his own. Being as his parents figured divorced people should never remarry, the lesser of two evils, apparently, was that he learn how to cook.

Honestly, he wouldn't mind learning a few things. But it was hard to accept his mother's help when she had that look on her face.

The five of them sat at the dinner table, and Cameron asked the blessing. His mom squirted ketchup on the boys' plates. Dad eyed the burger in front of him, sighed, and picked it up.

"So, boys, how was the summer program today?" Alaina seemed busy earlier when he picked the boys up. Not that it was her job to give him a daily report, but he'd missed the contact.

The twins eyed each other, neither saying a word.

Uh oh. That was usually a bad sign. "What did you do today, besides bring home this lettuce?"

Oliver elbowed Evan's arm, and Evan shoved back.

"Boys. What happened today?"

"Evan loves Ophelia," sang Oliver.

"Do not." By the ensuing scuffle, Evan had kicked Oliver under the table. With retaliation.

Cameron carefully avoided his parents' sharpened gazes and focused on the twins. He took a deep breath. "What do boys do when they like a girl?" Hopefully that was ambiguous enough that one of them would answer and provide some insight.

Oliver glanced at the adults around the table. "They might pull a girl's hair."

Mom made a slight gasping noise.

"That's not very nice." Although Cameron remembered doing that a time or two himself when he was a little tyke. No way could he allow a smile at this moment. "Anything else? Hypothetically, of course."

"They might throw crayons at them," Oliver continued earnestly. "Or they might push them. Just a little bit," he added quickly.

"I hope any sons of mine wouldn't do those things if they liked a girl. I hope they would be more respectful and not be mean."

The twins exchanged another look. They'd seemed to have a secret language practically since birth. Some days, Cameron wished he were on the inside track. Other times, he was just as glad it was all a mystery to him. "If you like a girl, it's okay to say that to her. Then you might want to share crayons instead of throwing them." He'd told Alaina he liked her. That had gone over much better than throwing frogs at her would have done. Not that he was going to have that particular discussion in front of his parents, even though it might help his sons.

"Miss Cheri made me say sorry." Evan's eyes flicked to his dad's.

Now they were getting somewhere. "I'm glad to hear that. You boys need to behave yourselves, because it's very hard to find someone to take care of you while Daddy is at work."

No sooner were the words out of his mouth than he regretted them. Talk about handing an opportunity to his mother on a silver platter.

She didn't let him down. "I'm happy to take over the boys' care." She gave them a stern look across the table. "I think it might do a world of good for two young gentlemen I know."

Four blue eyes widened. Two jaws dropped.

Cameron wasn't so sure about the world of good, but there was a certain amount of fear present. He might be able to put that to good use, but not at the moment. "We've got it covered, Mom. Let us work through this in our own way. Please."

Why didn't his father ever say anything? Didn't that go against the whole *man of the house* thing that had been instilled in Cameron as a child? Mind you, it had always been the case. Mom had ruled the roost, calling on Dad for backup as needed. Cameron couldn't fathom how their actions lined up with their words. A hands-on father would sure have helped him as a kid.

"Eat up your dinner, everyone." Not that he'd had more than a few French fries dunked in ketchup yet himself. The drive-through dinner really was rather lame. His mother had a point, though he would never admit it to her.

The big question was, could Alaina cook? And that brought up a second question, even bigger. Would his parents ever forgive him for remarrying? He was long past the age where he needed their permission for anything, but it would be really nice if they were on board.

Then he remembered that Alaina had stayed busy in her office when he picked up the boys today. Every other day she'd met him in the lobby and they'd chatted for a moment before he left. Cameron knew *he* was on board, but was Alaina having second thoughts?

Chapter 10

KENIA LOOKED UP from the stove as Alaina came in after work. "Hey, I hope you don't mind that I invited my brother and his new wife over for dinner tonight."

Mmm, the sautéing ground beef smelled good, but the last thing Alaina wanted was being around people she didn't know all that well. "Oh, I'm sorry. I'll find someplace to go." Maybe a trip into Twin Falls where she'd be less likely to see anyone who might feel sorry for her getting takeout on her own.

"Oh, that's not what I meant. You're welcome to stay and have dinner with us. I even tried a new recipe for those cloud thingies to have with strawberries and whipped cream." Kenia eyed her. "I really am sorry I sprang this on you. I should've at least called you at work."

Three weeks into the Grace Greenhouse summer program, Alaina had some sort of routine going on. What was in less of a routine was her relationship with Cameron. Who knew what was going on there? They'd been out about twice a week, and he'd never even tried to kiss her since that day at Evelyn and Ben's. Did that mean he regretted showing weakness — or whatever he might consider it — that day? Oh, they had nice dinners and long walks, but he was holding back. Maybe that was okay. Probably it was a good idea to get to know each other better before jumping in the deep end.

Problem was, Alaina's emotions were caught in a whirlpool. Why couldn't he just say something to clear the air? Of course, she should be talking to him about Evan's behavior, but the little guy had seemed to ease up on Ophelia the past few days, and Alaina didn't want to bring her day job up between them if she didn't have to.

"Alaina?"

Right. She hadn't answered her housemate. "Are you sure I won't be in the way? Extra wheel and all that?"

"No, I really want you to stay. I'm trying to make an effort with Grady, though we haven't ever been close. We're so far apart in age." Kenia eyed Alaina. "Well, I guess you know how that goes. You and Adriana are about the same. At any rate, I really like Joanna, and she's been good for my brother, so I want to try."

Grady. Joanna. She was Cameron's sister. How had Alaina forgotten even for a minute? She held up both hands as she stepped away. "Wait. No. Bad idea. I'm out of here."

"Don't be a chicken. Joanna's really nice. Pretty sure she won't bite."

"I don't want to find out. I'm dating her baby brother — sort of. And I don't know her at all."

Kenia's eyebrows shot up. "Sort of? I didn't think there was anything tentative about your relationship with Cameron."

He still hadn't invited her to spend any time with his parents. Mind you, she'd been just as reluctant to encourage her own parents to play nice. "It's complicated," she said at last.

"*It's complicated,*" mimicked Kenia. "That's a Facebook status designed for college kids who don't want to commit, not for adults who aren't dating exclusively."

"There's more than one way for things to be complicated. I don't know what Cameron has said to his sister about me, or if he's said anything at all."

The doorbell rang.

"Guess we'll find out soon enough, won't we?" Kenia stepped around Alaina to the door.

Not that Alaina was waiting around. She needed at least five minutes in her room to gather herself. It wasn't that Kenia hadn't thought about warning her. It was the fact her friend knew, given half a chance, that Alaina would find a way out. In her bedroom, she scanned herself in the full-length mirror and smoothed her hands down her striped top and khaki capris. Too casual? She'd thought they were okay for work, though. She loosened her hair and ran a brush through it before refastening the clip at her nape. This was as good as it was going to get. She beamed at herself in the mirror, practicing pretending this was going to be a great evening, before exiting her room.

Grady stood at the counter opening a can of refried beans while Joanna shredded cheese and Kenia stirred the ground beef in her frying pan. Kenia glanced up and winked. "Have you two met my roommate, Alaina Silva, yet? Grady, you probably remember her sister, Adriana, from high school."

The man turned and smiled. "I do remember Adriana, but I seem to recall you coming through the house with Kenia a time or two back then as well. Nice to meet you again."

This wasn't so bad. "Likewise. Yes, Kenia and I were in youth group together in high school."

"Alaina." Joanna's eyes twinkled. "If I remember correctly, you're the woman who monopolized my brother at our wedding reception a few weeks ago."

Uhhh. Words fled.

"And who's gone out with him half a dozen times since," Kenia put in. "Can you pass that packet of taco spice, please?"

"Don't let Joanna find out it isn't from scratch," Grady stage-whispered. "She tells me real, actual spices exist outside of foil packs."

For a second Alaina grasped the hope that Joanna would be diverted by the siblings' teasing, but she only glanced their way before looking back at Alaina.

"Interesting."

"Yeah, Evan and Oliver are in her program, too."

Thanks, Kenia. You can zip your face any minute now.

Grady looked over. "Oh, Cameron won that round? I thought your parents were determined to save him the money, Jo, and watch the twins this summer."

Everyone looked at Alaina, as though she had anything to do with it. She held up both hands. "The boys were pre-registered. Their grandmother has picked them up a few times, but it's usually Cameron."

Kenia snickered.

Alaina would ignore that. "What can I do to help?"

"I think we've got everything covered. I picked up some corn tortillas from Benita's Market after work, so we'll be assembling tostadas in just a minute."

"First packaged spices and now store-bought tortillas?" asked Grady with a mocking grin. "I promise I won't let the Quintanas know." He looked out the window. "Oh, wait — isn't that Veronica walking by? Does she know you're pretending to do it yourself when her family's Mexican restaurant is just a few blocks away?"

Kenia snapped her long-handled tongs in his direction. "Enough out of you, big brother. You're not the slightest bit amusing. I can cook better than our mother can."

If Alaina remembered correctly, the Akers family had always hired a chef, a housekeeper, and a groundskeeper. It had struck her funny bone that anyone in the garden business wouldn't do their own yard work.

"After all this time I've been after my brother to start dating again, I can't believe he did it when I wasn't looking." Joanna placed the bowl of shredded cheddar on the tiny counter beside Kenia and turned back to Alaina.

Grady smirked. "We were otherwise occupied."

"You can still take the credit." Kenia looked up from the stove.

"How so?"

"They met at your wedding, after all. It was Alaina who rescued Oliver from the goldfish pond."

"Oh, that wasn't me. Cameron hauled him out. I didn't really do anything."

"Those two are quite the pair, aren't they?" Joanna's eyebrows rose.

"Always in a scrape," Alaina agreed. "The thing is they aren't bad kids. They don't seem to be actually looking for trouble. Their bodies just move more quickly than their brains."

Kenia let loose an undignified snort. "I'm not so sure about that. It's not even possible two kids could be such trouble magnets if they weren't looking for it."

But Joanna's face softened into a smile. "I agree, Alaina. They're very sweet boys. I'm so glad I moved back to Arcadia Valley last year and got to know them while they're still so little. I only wish I'd come sooner."

"Me, too." Grady kissed his wife's cheek.

"Ha, if she'd come much earlier, you'd still have been wrapped up with Vanessa." Kenia grinned at her brother. "What was it Granddad always called her? Vanity?"

"I wouldn't have given Vanessa a second look once I met Joanna. My heart was waiting for her. I just didn't know it."

"Wow, bro. That's a lot of lovey-dovey mumbo-jumbo there."

"And it's all true." Grady pointed at the stove. "Shouldn't you be doing more stirring and less sniping? We wouldn't want dinner to burn. Although I hear El Corazon makes great tostadas. From scratch, even. We could walk over."

Kenia made a face and stirred the contents before sprinkling in the packaged spices. "Mmm, doesn't that smell good?" She added a bit of water and covered the wok. "Ready in five. Can you chop the avocado, Grady?"

A bit later the four of them sat around the tiny table with their dinner in front of them.

Grady asked the blessing before taking a bite. "Not bad for half-packaged," he teased.

Joanna had been rather quiet. Alaina felt the woman's gaze on her many times but, when she glanced over, Joanna was looking somewhere else. It was hard to believe Cameron hadn't said anything at all about her to his sister. On the other hand, the newlyweds had only been home for a few days. Maybe he hadn't had a chance when his parents or the twins weren't around.

The aromatic tostadas tasted flat. She and Cameron needed to talk. They needed to figure out how to get their parents on board... or else agree that neither of them cared what their parents thought. She needed to stop hiding in the office when he picked up the boys.

"The twins could really use some grounding in their lives," Joanna said into a lull in the conversation.

Everyone swung to look at her, including Alaina.

"They were so young when their mom left them." Joanna looked at Grady as though she were carefully avoiding Alaina. Maybe she was. "It's like they were new seedlings just beginning to sprout. Only a tiny root and no soil to dig it into. It's been tough for my brother. He's not really a nurturer. Boys in our family weren't taught to be. He was to provide the basics. The sunshine and rain, if you will. Lisa was to provide the gentle pruning. Instead, she yanked them out of their little garden bed and turned their roots up to wither, leaving Cameron to deal with the aftermath."

Why was Joanna explaining all this to Alaina? It was certain the other two at the table weren't the object of this lesson.

"I've told Cameron he should find someone." Joanna turned to Alaina now. "But, suddenly, I'm afraid of the twins getting hurt again, just when they're starting to adjust."

Alaina's back stiffened. "I would never damage them."

"Not on purpose, I'm sure." Joanna shook her head as though trying to dislodge unpleasant thoughts. "I'm sorry to be a downer. I want my brother to be happy. Trust me. I care about him a lot, but he's a big boy who makes his own decisions. It's the little boys I'm concerned about."

"Your parents don't think he should remarry." Alaina's eyes narrowed as she watched Cameron's sister.

"I know." She sighed. "You have to admit that the ideal is to marry once and build a strong marriage together."

Grady reached across the corner of the table and caressed one of Joanna's hands.

"I can agree with that, no problem. But life isn't always a fairy tale. Or, sometimes the fairy tale only comes once the evil godmother's spell is broken." Alaina's hand flew to cover her mouth. "Not that I'm calling Lisa evil."

Joanna let out a sardonic chuckle. "Trust me, she's been called worse. She always put herself before Cameron or the twins. I'm not saying she should have sacrificed everything for them. That's not healthy, either. But it was always all about her."

"Alaina's not like Lisa," put in Kenia.

"I'm sorry." Joanna gave Alaina a rueful grin. "This must have felt like it came out of nowhere. It wasn't my intention to cast a damper on anything. I tend to say what I'm thinking—"

"Does she ever!" interrupted Grady.

She wrinkled her nose at her husband before turning back to Alaina. "I want to be friends, but it's a bit conditional. If the boys love you, I'll love you."

"What about if Cameron loves her?"

Trust Kenia to come out with that one.

"My nephews come first. But I'm pretty sure Cameron wants what's best for his boys, too."

Was Alaina the best for all of them? Why was it so complicated? Right. Divorce took prisoners.

She nodded at Joanna. "Understood. I take it you don't share your parents' stance on remarriage."

"If you're asking if I think divorce is the unpardonable sin, the answer is no. I think God forgives us when we ask Him, no matter the situation, and gives us a clean slate. He gives us second chances. Even more, sometimes. But marriage is never something to be taken lightly, whether it's a first time or a second."

How on earth had she gotten into this conversation with Cameron's sister after fewer than a dozen dates? Who was thinking about weddings yet?

Okay, maybe in the wee hours of a sleepless night, she'd begun to let herself fantasize. Was that so wrong?

Chapter 11

CAMERON POKED HIS HEAD around Alaina's open office door. "Can we talk?"

She'd canceled their Tuesday night date, citing a headache, but that couldn't be all. She hadn't seemed herself for several days. Was she already rethinking their fledgling relationship after only a few short weeks?

Alaina looked up from her computer, a shaky smile lifting her lips. "I work until six."

His eyebrows rose. He knew that.

"Unless... is it about the boys?"

It wasn't about the boys unless she thought it was. "Is Evan causing trouble?"

The smile seemed a bit more genuine. "How come no one ever wonders if it's Oliver?"

Cameron chuckled, hoping it sounded natural. "Because it never is. But, no. I don't want to talk about the boys." He glanced around the lobby, but no one seemed to be paying attention to them, so he stepped deeper into the office. "I want to talk about us. I feel something's wrong, but I can't put my finger on it."

Her gaze flicked to the computer screen then out the window before dashing over his. "I'm at work."

"I know, but you canceled our date last night and didn't answer my text." He took a deep breath. "You have me worried."

"Don't be." She met his gaze and smiled, but the warmth and, yes, passion, she'd exhibited a week ago seemed to be missing.

"Having second thoughts?"

"Miss Alaina?" A woman's voice came from behind him.

Right. She kept telling him she was at work, and it was pickup time. He needed to respect that. He stepped aside.

Alaina brushed past him through the doorway, the skim of her arm against his causing a churning in his gut and a longing to gather her close.

"Yes?" she asked.

"Pippa and Tracy won't be in next week. Their grandparents will be in town for the Fourth of July."

"Will they be out of the program Monday through Friday?"

"Yes. Every day. Back the following Monday, though."

"Okay, good to know. I'll make a note of it."

"Thanks. Have a good Fourth!"

"I'm sure I will." Alaina turned back into her office and straight into him. "Excuse me."

Cameron steadied her, both hands on her upper arms. "Sorry for being in your way."

She looked away then stepped out of his hands. "You're not."

Could have fooled him. But if their relationship was doomed, he needed to know that sooner rather than later. Before he fell all the way in love with her.

The thought sloshed ice water over his heart. In love? Yeah, pretty much. He'd either been too slow letting her know, or maybe she felt like he was pushing her. Like he was right now. It was hard to know. Hard to read her. He backed up and leaned against the doorframe as she settled at her computer again.

"May I come back at six? I won't take up a lot of your time."

Alaina looked up, those gorgeous brown eyes colliding with his.

"Unless you want me to. Then we can spend the evening together."

Her gaze shuttered.

He'd done it again. But she needed to give him something to go on. Anything.

"Six. Okay."

"I'll be going then. Take the boys home. My mom won't mind taking care of things for a while." She might mind, but she'd do it anyway. The twins might mind, but they didn't get a say.

Alaina sucked in her lower lip but nodded.

Man, all he wanted to do was wipe that worried look from her face. He wanted to hold her close and kiss her. He'd almost done it that day at Ben and Evelyn's. Should he have? But not with three kids staring at them. He wanted their first kiss to be memorable.

Yeah, they'd gone out a couple of times since, but she'd

seemed a bit more reserved, and he hadn't wanted to push her. They really hadn't known each other long. Not even an entire month, yet.

But his heart knew where it belonged. Did hers?

"Miss Alaina?" said someone from behind him.

Cameron nodded at Alaina. "See you soon." This time he managed to escape the office, find his sons, and get all the way out of the greenhouse parking lot.

Alaina locked up the children's center just as Cameron's car pulled back into the yard. How could she feel this messed up inside? How could she want him so desperately and feel compelled to push him away at the same time? He wasn't like Garth. She wasn't on the rebound. It had been seven and a half months since that relationship ended.

Then why? Was it Joanna's warning? She'd been over it and over it through long days and endless nights.

Cameron walked toward her. Man, he looked good in those cargo shorts and red T-shirt, his hair damp as though he'd just stepped from the shower. Where had he found the time?

Concern and hope warred on his face.

Her fault. She moved toward him to the edge of the deck.

Cameron stopped on the top step, putting him nearly at eye level. He was so near she could smell his aftershave, feel the warmth radiating from his body.

She shivered slightly, her eyes refusing to leave the pull of his. *Get it together, girl. The issues are real.* Her brain might as well be shouting down the hollow pipeline into Twitter for all the good it did. Her eyes weren't listening. Neither was her heart. Or her pulse.

"Hi." *Brilliant opening, Alaina.*

"Hi." His gaze softened. "Want to go for a walk from here, or shall we go for a drive?"

A drive would be safer. His hands would be occupied with the car. They'd be separated by the console.

"Let's walk." Yeah, her brain and her mouth really needed to start communicating.

He held his hand out to her, and she took it, feeling the warm, strong clasp as they descended the few steps.

"Is your headache gone?" he asked, glancing down at her as their arms brushed.

"My head—?" Right. That was the excuse she'd given him a couple of days back. "Kind of." True enough. Nothing that a solid sleep wouldn't cure, most likely, if she ever had a good night again.

"I'm sorry it's been bothering you."

"Yeah. It comes and goes."

They ambled past the long garden beds where a few volunteers pulled weeds. Looked like another bumper crop year for the charity Ben and Evelyn operated, feeding the homeless. At least Maisie wasn't there just now. That kid certainly wouldn't miss their entwined hands.

"I wasn't sure if it was me. If I'd caused you to have second thoughts."

Here came the moment of truth. It hovered in front of her, but Alaina could find no words. Half a dozen responses burned through her mind, discarded just as quickly.

"*Are* you having second thoughts?" His voice was so quiet she strained to hear it.

Alaina took a long breath and let it out slowly. "A little? I'm confused. I'm not sure what's the best thing."

His fingers squeezed hers. "Okay, I get that. What are the confusing bits? Can we talk about them?"

She might as well be back in college psych class. "It's complicated." But she needed to try, right? Otherwise she might as well kiss him goodbye right here and now. She wanted to kiss him, all right, but not goodbye. She wanted to kiss him 'hello, where have you been all my life?'

They rounded the end of the block and strolled down a residential street, shaded with huge overhanging trees. Small but tidy yards with riotous flowerbeds lined the sidewalk, filling the air with fragrant perfume in the gentle breeze. A few birds flitted from tree to tree, and a hummingbird drank deeply from a feeder on a front porch.

Here went nothing. "I like you, Cameron. I-I like you a lot." She might even be tumbling into love, but surely a few weeks wasn't long enough to know. She'd been way too quick to claim that status with Garth, and look where it had gotten her.

"I like you, too." Cameron's voice was low. Husky. His fingers gripped hers so tightly she might never have sensation again.

"I don't know. Is it enough? My parents are unhappy about us, and so are yours. Your mom said—" Drat, she hadn't meant to go there.

Cameron looked down at her. "My mother has been talking to you?"

Alaina let out a breath. "She's picked up the boys a couple of times."

"Right. When I had to work late."

She nodded. "She didn't say much to me, but I overheard her talking to Nancy Poncetta — she was there picking up Ophelia and Isabella — about the sanctity of marriage and how divorce grieves God. I'm pretty sure I was meant to overhear."

Cameron mumbled something under his breath that she couldn't quite catch. Maybe it was just as well. Then his arm wrapped around her waist and he pulled her close to his side. "A lot of things grieve God. Every lie, every selfish thought, every time pride gets the best of us. We put things in a hierarchy, but God doesn't. He says we all sin. We all miss the mark."

"For all have sinned and fall short of the glory of God," Alaina whispered.

"Exactly. And in Matthew, Jesus says thinking about murdering someone is as bad as doing it. Lust is as bad as adultery. When we start comparing ourselves to God's standards, we don't come up smelling like roses. None of us, my parents included."

The words made so much sense. But still. "It's complicated, regardless. You've been married. You haven't said much, but I assume you still hear from your ex. You have kids."

"Lisa doesn't call often, and when she does, it's for the boys. I'd like to deny them contact, but she *is* their mother."

"Exactly. That's what I'm trying to say. They have a mom. They don't nee—"

Cameron turned to face her. "They *do* need. You see them every day. The more love and care poured out on them, the better off they'll be."

His hand lifted and slid gently down her cheek, caressing her jaw. "They're not the only ones who need love."

She stared into his brown eyes, glittering dangerously mere inches away. She wasn't ready for the L word. Not that he'd quite given it. In context, she had to agree. "I know," she whispered.

"Alaina, we haven't known each other long. I know it's too soon to be thinking of forever."

She wanted forever. See? She couldn't make up her mind. When they were apart, the rational, logical reasons of why this was a bad idea held sway. When they were together — especially when he looked at her this way — she knew this could be her forever love. But she'd thought that before, with Garth, so how could she know for sure? And then there was Lisa.

"But, if you're willing, I want to move forward in faith. That we'll talk to each other, that we'll share our misgivings, that we'll work through things together. If our relationship is not going to work with all that, I think God will show us."

Alaina sucked in her lower lip. That made sense. She'd never know if she kept putting up premature boundaries. If she didn't give it her all. If he was willing to, why wasn't she? She nodded slowly.

Cameron's other hand rose and, between them, they held her face ever so gently. His gaze, intensifying, dropped to her lips.

This was it. Last chance to run.

She tipped her face toward his and closed her eyes as her hands rested on his hips.

His soft lips brushed over hers, the tingle exploding into fireworks through her entire body. Then he closed in with more promise, capturing her and all her senses in one bold, deep kiss.

Alaina wrapped her arms around his waist, holding him close as their lips tasted each other, savored each other, melded together. Her hands roamed up to smooth the muscles in his back, his strong shoulders.

The kiss went on until her emotions sang in unison.

Yes, this was the man for her. Everything they'd talked about — all the obstacles in their path — could wait. Would be taken care of in their own time.

For now, only she and Cameron existed, wrapped in each other's arms, trusting. Oh, yes. Trusting.

Chapter 12

NO, YOU AND DAD can't ride with me. I'm picking Alaina up."

Cameron's mother pursed her lips. "But you said there's limited parking."

He *had* mentioned that, hadn't he? "Let me give Joanna a call and see if she and Grady can swing by for you." It was the Fourth of July, and he and Alaina were getting their families together for the first time. This was either going to be a fantastic evening or an utter failure. Barry and Linda Akers probably didn't care about him and Alaina one way or the other, but his parents and Alaina's certainly had opinions. It was time — probably past time — to get everyone together and see how it went.

Mom shook her head. "Not in that silly car of Grady's. I'm not a pretzel to get in the backseat of that."

Cameron tried to wipe the grin away before it got going. Grady's sporty Eos was definitely made for two people. When Joanna got pregnant — and Cameron hoped it would be soon; his sister was already thirty-one — Grady would need to buy something more practical.

Mom sighed. "Fine. We'll drive over ourselves. Where are we going again?"

"Arcadia Creek Park. Just go north to Main Street, turn left, and follow the signs. You'll see it."

His mother pursed her lips. "Fine, but…"

"One more thing?"

Her eyebrows rose.

"Please give Alaina a chance. She's special."

"You do know what your father and I believe."

He bit back a sarcastic response about how he would never be able to guess. "I know. All I'm asking you to do is be nice. You can pray all you want. In fact, I hope you are. I sure am."

"You can't just say the words, son. You have to mean them. You have to really want God to show you and then be obedient."

Cameron kept his smile steady. "God knows my heart. He's drawn me so close to Himself in the past three years. There's no way I want to give that up. Not for Alaina. Not for anyone."

She frowned. "Then…?"

He leaned over and kissed her cheek. "I'll see you at the park in half an hour, okay? I've got our share of the food and gear."

After all this time, the twins had disappeared again. "Evan! Oliver!" he hollered. "Time to go."

They came running around the corner of the house, shoving at each other.

"Hands to yourself." He opened the car door and they

clambered in. "Seatbelts. Let's go."

"When will I be big enough to sit in the front?" whined Evan.

Cameron glanced in the rearview mirror. Good. They might be grouching, but they were buckling up. "Not for a long time. When you're a teenager." His gut soured at the thought of them that age.

"When's that?"

"You'll be seven in a few weeks. You do the math." He pulled away from the curb.

"After that we'll be eight," said Oliver.

"Then nine," responded Evan.

They alternated and tried to figure out the answer. By the time they'd decided it was twelve years in the future — a number Cameron approved of, though the accountant in him quailed — he'd pulled into the circle drive at Valley Cottages.

Evan perked up. "Hey, where are we?"

"This isn't the park," announced Oliver.

"We're going to give Miss Alaina a ride."

"But why?" Evan, of course.

"Because she's really nice. What do you think?"

The boys looked at each other as he put the car in Park. "She has pretty hair," said Oliver.

"Agreed. Now stay buckled up, you hear?" Cameron hurried to the front steps.

Alaina opened the door before he could knock. Oliver hadn't said the half of it. More than Alaina's hair was pretty — although pulled back into a long braid, it was definitely eye-catching under a wide-brimmed white hat. She wore a pair of gray shorts and a flag-themed tank top with red flip-flops on her feet.

Cameron steadied himself against the porch post. "You look amazing," he managed to get out.

She grinned. "You look pretty good yourself."

"You're the flower and I'll be your leaves." Where had that come from? Sappy.

Alaina tipped her head back and laughed. Then she reached for a straw beach bag and tucked her other hand into his.

"So long as our roots are digging deep and we're getting sunshine and rain, we should be good to go then."

Huh. Maybe not too sappy after all. "Is there anything else that needs to come?"

"No, my parents are bringing lawn chairs and two ice chests full of food. Maybe three, so I'm off the hook."

Cameron popped the trunk open and set her bag inside before rounding the car and opening the passenger door.

She settled in and turned. "Hi, boys."

"Hi, Miss Alaina," they chorused.

Cameron grinned as he walked around to the driver's side, waving at Veronica Quintana as she exited a cottage a few doors down. She waved back. He slid into the car.

"How come you're coming with us?" asked Oliver.

"Dad said she had pretty hair," said Evan.

Alaina's eyes laughed at him across the front of the car.

Cameron shrugged and chuckled. "Ollie said it first." He winked. "I just agreed with him."

Alaina angled in the seat. "Did your dad tell you that my nephew and niece will be at the picnic today?"

"No." Evan glared at Cameron via the mirror. "How old are they?"

"Sam is ten and Violet is eight."

"How come they're not our age?"

"Because they were born before you were."

"Oh." Evan appeared to be thinking that one over. "How come the girl is closer to our age? I want the boy to be."

"I think you'll like playing with Violet. She's like Maisie."

Oliver's face brightened. "Dad, will Maisie and her parents be there?"

Cameron turned the car onto the highway. "They sure will. Everyone will be there."

"Everyone?" asked Evan. "Even Ophelia? I don't want her to be."

"How about Mommy? She's part of everyone." Oliver sounded wistful.

Alaina's lips lost their upward tilt.

So did Cameron's.

Everyone turned out to be a lot of people. Alaina had known it would be, but nerves clawed at her as she looked around the loose circle. She'd already been nervous before Oliver asked about Lisa, but that hadn't helped, not even a little bit.

"You've met Granddad, haven't you?" Kenia pushed a wheelchair down the paved path toward them, its occupant a long, thin man with a shock of white hair and startling blue eyes.

"I sure have. Good to see you again, Mr. Akers."

His bushy brows furrowed as he focused on her, but his face brightened when he noticed the boys.

"Granddad!" they shouted, running toward the wheelchair. They flung themselves at the man. "Is it your birthday again?"

Alaina winced, hoping Kenia had the contraption steady, but her friend was good for it. The old man's eyes clouded as he twisted to see Kenia. "Is it?'

"Not today. It's the Fourth of July, remember?" She waggled her finger at the twins. "But don't worry. There will be cake and ice cream."

"Yay!" They scrambled toward Maisie, who sprawled beside Evelyn and Ben on a picnic blanket.

Holding his hand, Alaina pulled Cameron toward her family. She'd already met his and didn't need his mother to scowl at her anymore. "Cameron, I'd like you to meet my sister, Adriana. This is her husband, Myles, and her kids, Sam and Violet. Adriana and Myles, this is... Cameron." Gah. Why hadn't she thought how the introduction should go? Did she call him her boyfriend? It would have been a safe designation, considering the kissing they'd done. Oh, well, too late for a redo.

Cameron's left hand slipped around her waist as he shook Adriana's hand then Myles's. "Pleased to meet you both. Alaina has told me a lot about you." He waved toward the twins. "Those rascals are my sons, Oliver and Evan."

The two pelted Maisie with handfuls of grass. Alaina

glanced at her sister's kids. Both Violet and Sam watched with interest. "The girl is Maisie, a friend of ours. She's eleven."

"She looks nice," announced Violet. "She's going to be my friend." She strode over to where the threesome played, Sam tagging at her heels.

"Good for Violet." Alaina smiled at her sister.

"Alaina tells me you live in Spokane," Cameron was saying to Myles. "What do you do there?"

"I teach second grade at Bridgeview Elementary. And you?"

"I'm an accountant at Stargil, a manufacturing plant at the south end of Arcadia Valley. We specialize in potato products."

"I've heard of Stargil potato chips." Myles nodded.

Adriana glanced between them. "Does it ever bother you to work in industrial food?"

Uh oh. Alaina closed her eyes for a second.

Cameron's arm tightened around Alaina's waist. "It's a good job and pays well. If I don't do it, someone else will."

"Our whole community in Bridgeview has been getting more and more into locally grown food." Adriana tucked her hand into Myles's. "We've got a community garden now, and the beginnings of a permaculture food forest. The elementary school just completed the first year of integrating a gardening program into the curriculum."

Myles nodded. "Don't forget Peter Santoro's new market garden, as well." He chuckled. "I'd never have thought, a year ago, that I'd be such a proponent of growing food, but Adriana made a believer out of me."

"It helps that she's such a good cook," put in Alaina. Diverting the conversation could only be good. "I need to get some recipes from you, sis. Now that I have access to so many fresh vegetables through the greenhouse project, it's time to up my game."

Adriana's face lit. "We'd love to have a tour while we're in town. It's such an amazing opportunity."

"Sure, come around at six when I'm off work. Or talk to Maisie. She can show you around anytime now that school is out for the summer."

Her sister frowned and glanced over at the children. "Maisie?"

"She's the instigator of the whole project," Cameron put in, pride in his voice. "She had the idea, rounded up dozens of volunteers, and is still the hardest worker on the property well into our second year."

"That kid? Over there?"

Maisie tickled a giggling Evan, who begged for mercy.

"Yep, that one."

"Wow."

Alaina felt a surge of pride at being part of something that elicited any awe from her big sister. All her life, it had been the other way around. Adriana marrying her college sweetheart, Stephan, giving birth to two darling children — though Violet soon proved to be a handful — managing to pull herself together after her husband's noble death, then meeting and marrying Myles this past year.

Meanwhile, Alaina had just muddled along, earned her degree, worked at one daycare after another, and been involved with a man who'd rather be with someone else.

She shook herself. That was all history. Now she had a great job back in Arcadia Valley and a boyfriend who adored her. Right. A boyfriend who was divorced and had two kids, something her parents kept mentioning. She still couldn't measure up to her perfect big sister, but at least Adriana hadn't made a big deal about Cameron's marital status when they'd had a heart-to-heart over the phone. She'd asked about it, sure, but seemed satisfied with Alaina's reply.

A small distance away, Ben surged to his feet. "Looks like it's time for the ball game. Who's going to play for Grace Fellowship?"

Grady, lounging on a blanket with his head in Joanna's lap, opened one eye. "Are you kidding me? AV Community has Alex Quintana. We don't stand a chance."

"Says you."

"Says everyone. He was a star in the major leagues."

Ben planted both hands on his hips. "Chicken."

"Go ahead, man. Be my guest."

Ben shook his head. "Cameron? Myles?"

Cameron looked down at her. "Want to come play?"

She blinked. "Is it co-ed?"

He shrugged. "I think so. It was last year." He raised his voice. "And, for the record, last year AVCC only won by a handful of runs."

Grady didn't move. "Quintana was still recovering from that shoulder injury."

"We've got the Baxter brothers, and they look athletic," added Ben. "Who's in?"

Myles glanced at Adriana. "I play ball."

She grinned. "Go for it."

"If you want to play, Cameron, the twins are fine with me." Joanna's hand swept Grady's hair off his forehead. "Doesn't look like I'm going anywhere."

"Sure. It's a while until we eat anyway, right?"

At Joanna's nod, Alaina allowed Cameron to lead her away, falling into step with Ben, Adriana, and Myles. Maybe she was being a fraidy-cat not to stick around with her parents' generation. Well, so be it. There was a long evening ahead of them yet.

They neared the ball diamond where the fireworks would be set off later. Right now, men and women warmed up, playing catch and testing bats.

She wasn't going to play. Not if they weren't in dire need of more bodies in the outfield. She'd seen Alex Quintana play back in high school, and she wasn't about to pit herself against any team he was on.

Cheering for Cameron and the other Grace Fellowship players? That she could do.

Chapter 13

GROANING, CAMERON FLOPPED to the grass beside Alaina. "My legs. I'm dying."

She smoothed the short hair on his forehead. "That was a good hit."

"Straight down the third baseline." Man, he'd tried to angle himself to slam the ball closer to center field, but he'd been lucky to hit it at all. Of course Quintana was everywhere, but did Cameron have to plunk the ball straight at the former major league player?

"Two out." Alaina chewed her lip.

Quintana fired the ball at second, where Andrew Bigby tagged Jonah Baxter out. Now Ben stood at the plate, flexing the bat and staring down the pitcher from Arcadia Valley Community.

"Go, Ben!" shouted Alaina. Others took up the chant.

A ball arrowed across the plate.

"Strike one!" yelled the ump.

"Who's that?" asked Alaina.

"Silas Black, from Holy Trinity. A volunteer from every team is on umpire rotation." Cameron nudged her. "He's married to your friend."

"I know." Alaina shoved his shoulder. "Like I care."

"Strike two!"

Cameron was missing the action and couldn't bring himself to care as he looked up at Alaina, blocking the sun with her large hat. So pretty. So nice. Could it really be true?

Cra-ack!

Alaina jumped to her feet, and Cameron's head slammed the ground. He rolled over to see Ben sprinting for first base.

The small crowd yelled, some encouraging Ben and some screaming for Brooke Lockwood to catch the pop fly. She missed and the ball bounced, with her scrambling after it.

Ben rounded second base and headed for third, glancing over his shoulder. The second baseman caught Brooke's throw and arrowed it at Quintana. Ben slid, connecting with the base just as the ball jammed into Quintana's glove.

"Safe!"

Myles stepped up to bat, taking a few practice swings. He swung at the first pitch, slamming a grounder past the startled short stop and sprinting for first base. The infielder fired the ball at home, but Ben slid in with a split second to spare.

"Yay!" Alaina jumped, double high-fiving her sister. "Now we're only three runs behind."

When the game was over, AVCC had only beat them by one run. It was a good thing Myles was athletic and had agreed to play for Grace Fellowship, or Alaina wasn't sure what would've happened. Not that it was the end of the world, of course. She'd seen a new side of Cameron, a side where he could be competitive, where he could laugh, where he could taunt Andrew Bigby and laugh with Luke Delis. So many people she'd forgotten even existed since she moved away ten years ago, like Andrew Bigby, though he'd been a few years ahead of her. Seemed he'd moved back permanently to care for his grandmother. She couldn't help wondering who else had returned.

A piercing scream reverberated through the air.

Cameron angled his head for one brief instant, listening, then grabbed her hand. "Come on!" He took off running, dragging her behind him.

What on earth? Had that been one of the twins?

Moments later they raced into the area where their parents and the younger kids had been left. Both of Cameron's twins peered up a tree. The preschool teacher in Alaina did a quick head count. "Where is Violet?"

Evan pointed upward. "Way up there!" His blue eyes were round with awe.

"Who screamed?" Cameron looked between his sons. "It sounded like you." He pointed a finger at Oliver.

The little guy crossed his hands over his chest and shook his head. "No, Dad. It was Violet."

By now, everyone was back from the game. Alaina looked around. Myles hurried to the base of the tree and peered up. "Violet? What are you doing up there?"

A timid voice — one Alaina did not usually correspond with her adventuresome niece — came from above. "They said a girl couldn't climb a tree. I just wanted to show them."

Myles drew Adriana to his side as they looked up. "Well,

I guess you've proved your point. So come on down now, because it is almost time for the picnic."

"But I can't."

"What do you mean, you can't?" asked Adriana.

"My foot is stuck."

Evan gazed upward. "She was way up at the very top." His voice was shrouded in awe. "So high that the tree began to bend, and she fell a little, but then she caught herself on another branch." He looked up at Cameron, his eyes shining. "It was awesome."

Myles shot an irritated look at Evan. Alaina could hardly blame him. This kid was a lot of trouble at times. She should know. Visions of an angry Ophelia dashed through her head.

Cameron let go of Alaina's hands, crouched down, and wrapped an arm around each twin, drawing them aside he pinned a look on Evan. "Why were you so mean to Violet?"

Behind her, Alaina could hear Myles trying to talk Violet down the tree, but all of Alaina's focus was on Cameron and his sons. Sure, she knew his kids were a handful. But they hadn't spent a lot of time together, all four of them. Usually his parents kept the twins while they went out on a date. Why would they even do that, when they so obviously didn't think Cameron should remarry? It wasn't anything personal against her — at least, she didn't think so.

"Did you tell her girls can't climb trees?"

"Yeah, he said that." Oliver leaned against Cameron's shoulder. "And she yelled at him and said she could, too."

That proclamation wouldn't impress Violet a whole lot. She was too much like Evan, bouncing from one near accident to the next. Only, most adults found Evan endearing, while they spoke of Violet more in terms of obstinate and unyielding.

"Come on down, honey," Adriana soothed. "You've got this."

Violet's whimper came from up above.

Alaina turned just as Myles jumped for the bottom branch and swung himself up. "I'm coming, sweetie."

Myles had stepped right into the role of being a dad for Violet and Sam. If she kept seeing Cameron, if she married him — although that seemed a crazy thought the moment — could she do this good of a job as stepparent to Oliver and Evan? She'd have to talk to Myles later. Get some tips from him, maybe. Now he carefully tested the branches as he climbed, talking to Violet as he went.

Alaina glanced at her sister. Adriana stood, both hands pressed against the tree trunk, gazing upward with rapt concentration. Then Alaina looked back at Cameron, kneeling between his twins. The low murmur of his voice confirmed he had the situation under control. Not that there was anything she could do. She looked around, realizing for the first time that Sam and Maisie weren't there. Neither were her parents. Only Barry and Linda Akers and Cameron's parents watched, but seemed mostly focused on chatting with each other. Kenia must have taken Granddad for a walk somewhere in his wheelchair.

"I've got you," came Myles's voice from above. "I won't let you fall. Just put your foot right here on this branch... this foot, the one I'm touching."

Branches rustled overhead, and she heard a little gasp.

"It's okay, sweetie. I've got you. Now move your hand

to that other branch. Your left hand."

Everywhere she looked, Alaina felt like a fifth wheel. No wonder Myles had won Mom and Dad over. He was awesome. He'd given himself completely, not only to Adriana, but also to her children. Alaina got that. Really, she did. He was not only Adriana's husband, but had fully taken responsibility as Sam and Violet's dad. Stephan would never walk in the door again. He would never taunt Myles and tell them to back off and leave his kids alone. No, if people could look down from heaven — something that might not be all that scriptural — he would be asking God to bless Myles, thankful that his family had found another champion.

Lisa would so not be like that. And the odds of her coming around from time to time were high. Alaina's gut clenched. Was that why everything still felt so surreal? Could she really be the kind of stepparent to Oliver and Evan that Myles was to Sam and Violet?

A few hours later the group reassembled over at the ball diamond. Hundreds of residents of Arcadia Valley settled on the bleachers, on lawn chairs, and on blankets, waiting for the fireworks to begin. Holding Alaina's hand, Cameron sat down with his back pressed up against a tree. He was about to tug her into place between his raised knees, leaning against his chest, when two small tornadoes scrambled in more quickly than she did.

Oomph. Those little elbows were sharp.

He looked up at Alaina, still standing beside him. She looked at him, but her face was in the shadow, and he couldn't see her expression. He could imagine it, though. He gave her hand a little pull. "Sit beside me?"

She lowered herself to the ground beside him, wrapping both arms around her knees as she drew them to her chest. Barely a whisper would fit between them, but this was not the way he'd imagined it. Still, he was a father, first. He sure didn't want the boys running wild in the dark with fireworks about to go off. He tucked one arm around them, like closing the portable gate when they'd been little. He wrapped his other arm around Alaina, nestling her a little closer to his side. "Not quite what I had in mind," he whispered.

She glanced at him, but he still couldn't read her face. He rubbed her shoulder and upper arm, catching his fingers in her long, tangled curls. She'd worn her hair pulled back all day, but a few tendrils had managed to escape. Why wouldn't she relax against him?

"Alaina?" Her sister's voice.

She turned away as her sister and brother-in-law settled on the grass beside her. Maybe he was reading too much into this. It wasn't as though he shouldn't have expected the twins to wiggle in between his knees first. They were quick little guys.

Alaina and her sister spoke quietly to each other. Cameron couldn't quite make out their words, but Adriana glanced his way. He thought he saw a smile on her face, but he couldn't be sure.

Boom! The first fireworks blasted into the sky with an explosion of red glittering lights.

Oliver's hands came up to cover his ears, his little elbows sticking straight out to either side. Evan shoved at his twin's arm. "Ouch. Dad, he poked me."

One of these years, Cameron would remember to bring earmuffs for the twins. Not that Evan was likely to wear them, of course, but Oliver might.

He tried to get a little more comfortable, but a knot in the tree dug into his back. Wasn't that just the way? His hand caressed Alaina's arm. This time she seemed to settle against him a little more. He'd take that. He pressed a kiss to her temple, and she turned to look up at him. He'd like to kiss her lips, but could he reach with the twins pinning him down?

Boom! A second set of fireworks feathered sparkling lights across the sky.

He saw the reflection in Alaina's eyes as she looked up at him. He'd only caught the sight out of his peripheral vision himself. It looked like she might be just as distracted as he was. Once more, he nuzzled the side of her head. This time, she tipped her face upward to receive his kiss on her lips.

Boom! Boom! Boom!

Were all those fireworks just for this moment? He caressed her lips with his own, not quite being able to reach the depths he would've liked, but maybe that was just as well.

Evan's elbow dug into the soft flesh of Cameron's thigh. "Dad? What are you doing?"

Caught. Caught between his young sons' questions and the glimmer he caught in Alaina's eyes as another explosion shattered the air.

Oliver wiggled. "What do you mean, what is Dad doing?" He paused for a second. "Oh."

The twins would need to know sooner or later anyway, right? Cameron snuggled both boys against his chest. They were having none of that nonsense. Both struggled for a little more space as they turned to look at him and Alaina.

Cameron looked from one boy to the other. "What was I doing? I was kissing Miss Alaina."

Another ear-shattering explosion rocked the ball diamond, but Cameron had no eyes to see the beauty that was surely flashing through the sky above them. Not when he could see the reflection in Alaina's eyes as she looked between the twins and him.

"I told you two monkeys that I like Miss Alaina. A lot. She is someone special to me."

What, silence? Since when was Evan rendered speechless? Even Oliver, although he seemed poised to say something, remained silent.

"Turn around, boys. You don't want to miss the rest of the fireworks."

With another searching tilt of the head, the boys settled back between his knees, Oliver with his hands over his ears once again. At least now he had his elbows tucked in.

Cameron pressed Alaina's head against his shoulder and kissed her hair. "That went over better than I thought it might," he murmured.

He felt a shudder passed through her, and he kept his hand moving down her head through her hair, down her shoulder, down her arm. A second later another explosion with the sky this one in red, white, and blue.

"Matches your tank top," he whispered. "Have I told you yet today how beautiful you are?"

He felt her nod against his shoulder, but she didn't turn to look at him again. Something was going on in her mind. He didn't know what. It had come and gone for the better part of a week, but he had thought he'd set it to rest the other day when they'd gone for a walk in the neighborhood near the greenhouses. Apparently not — not completely, anyway. But if she were content to stay nestled against his shoulder for now, he'd accept that.

Cameron's gut clenched. He'd been so stupid with Lisa, thinking she was going to be the one he would spend the rest of his life with. He'd known she wasn't a believer, but it hadn't mattered to him as much as it should have. She'd been fun, the life of the party, and she'd loved him. She'd introduced him to a whole new world that he hadn't even known existed before she'd swept into his life. If only he could do those years over again, and hold out for someone as sweet as Alaina. Someone who loved the Lord.

The twins shot pointy elbows at each other, and his hand automatically soothed them without conscious thought. So, yes, it would have been better to not get mixed up with Lisa. But then, these precious little boys would never have come into his life. They certainly kept him on his toes and then some, but that wasn't all bad. They had taught him a lot about love, the kind that was always there because of one's relationship with someone. Not something that needed to be earned every five minutes, like it seemed he needed to do with Lisa. Just love that *was*, no matter what.

He was falling in love with Alaina. He was pretty sure she was falling in love with him, too. But, while he felt she would make his life complete, she'd get a ready-made family.

Probably no woman really wanted that. Who was he to think that he was such a great catch that she'd overlook the fact that he came with two rambunctious boys?

More and more explosions rocked the night air, sending showers of cascading light over the entire area. This was how he'd felt since Alaina came into his life. At first just a small spark or two, but the flares of attraction were stronger now, bigger, louder, harder to ignore. Not that he wanted to ignore her.

With the final crescendo, the fireworks were over. Cheers, clapping, and whistling sounded all around them as Arcadia Valley residents sent their appreciation to the town.

"That was amazing," breathed Evan.

Oliver took his hands away from his ears. "Is it over?"

Cameron chuckled. "Yes, it's over for another year. We're going to head back to the car now. You two stick tight and don't run off." Thankfully he'd carted all the picnic paraphernalia to the car earlier.

"Yes, Daddy."

He managed to raise himself to standing around their little bodies then pulled Alaina up beside him. He glanced at the two boys, then at Alaina. There was no way he wanted one of the twins to come between them. "Ollie, would you please hold Miss Alaina's hand? Evan, hold mine."

Obedient for once, Oliver stepped to the other side of Alaina, and her fingers closed around his son's. This was going to work. "Okay everyone, back to the car. It's way past your bedtime. I hope it was worth it."

The overhead lights above the ball diamond had been slowly brightening as they gathered themselves together. The two little guys looked more energized than tired, but Cameron could only hope they'd crash as soon as they tumbled into their beds. He slipped his arm around Alaina's waist, and felt a rush of pleasure when her hand went around his back. He felt her thumb hook through his belt loop. "Let's go, then."

Chapter 14

ER SISTER SAT CROSS-LEGGED on the bed
across from Alaina, a bowl of popcorn between them.
"So tell me about Mr. Gorgeous."

Alaina had known this was coming, but better in her
room at the cottage than in their parents' house where Mom
might want in on the conversation. Or Myles, or one of the
kids. "I'm not sure where to start."

"Are you in love?" Adriana gathered a few kernels of
popcorn in her hand.

"I don't know. Maybe? It's too soon to be sure."

"It kind of sneaks up on a person. Or it did me. Myles
says he knew almost right away that I was the woman for
him."

Her sister had said the same about Stephan years ago, too.
How did one woman get to be so fortunate, finding love with

two good men? Not that it had been lucky to have her first husband die.

Adriana eyed her. "If you're not sure you're in love, what do you feel for him?"

"He's nice. I like him a lot. He's sweet and attentive. But..."

"But what?"

Alaina sighed. "He's divorced."

"So you've said."

"How can you say it like that? Don't you care?"

"I'm not sure what you mean. Of course I care. You're my baby sister and I want you to be happy."

"Mom and Dad think it's a big deal. You should hear them go on and on."

Adriana chuckled.

"Maybe you did hear it, when we went to play ball."

"Nope, they didn't say a thing then. Mostly just glowered at Cameron's parents until Sam got Dad to play catch with him and Maisie. She seems a good kid."

"She is. I don't know her well, but her mom is my boss."

"Cool. But back to our parents. You know they're fiercely protective of their daughters." Adriana toggled her thumb back and forth between them.

Alaina rolled her eyes. "As though we were still twelve."

"Yeah, that." Adriana grinned. "You'll remember they didn't think Myles was the right man for me just last Christmas."

"I know, but he wasn't *divorced*."

Adriana gave her a steady look. "No, he wasn't. But Dad will always err on the side of caution, and with Violet reacting so badly to finding out her mom and her teacher were dating, Dad felt he was doing the right thing to side with the kids."

"Because you were obviously so infatuated you didn't even think of how this affected your children." Alaina couldn't keep the frustration out of her voice. At least with her big sister, she didn't need to pretend.

"I know, right? They'd decided I was a responsible adult years ago, but one tiny slip in judgment — in their opinion — and *bam*! It was like I was the kid again."

Alaina grabbed a pillow and scrunched it tight to her stomach. "But you knew the problem would go away in time. Plus, you didn't even live here. If I'd have known I'd meet Cameron, I'm not sure I would've moved back to Arcadia Valley. There's nothing in the world like dating under your parents' noses when you're an adult."

"But if you hadn't moved back, you wouldn't even have met him."

"I know." Alaina sucked in her lower lip. "And then I wouldn't be so confused."

"Okay, back up a bit. I thought you said you might be in love with him. Would you really rather not have met him at all?"

Alaina could be thankful her sister wasn't pushing her to declare feelings she wasn't sure she had. She squeezed the pillow tighter. "I know that sounds ridiculous. It's just that... he's divorced."

"You mentioned that. Tell me why it matters."

"I told you about it on the phone last week." Not every-thing, though.

"I know. But it's still bugging you, so talk already."

Alaina sighed. "This is going to sound terrible."

Her sister's lips quirked up at the corners. "I'll be the judge of that."

"For Mom and Dad, it's that Cameron is divorced. While I don't love that part myself, I can't really hold it against him. His ex left him, and it's been a few years. A few years where he's been growing as a Christian. So, as far as I'm concerned, the divorce is water under the bridge."

"Okay." Adriana nodded. "So far, so good."

Alaina took a deep breath. "For me, the bigger problem is his kids." When her sister didn't speak right away, Alaina peered up through her lashes. "Don't hate me. I've always wanted to be a mom, but being a stepmother never figured in my dreams."

"They're active little boys." It seemed Adriana picked her words carefully. "You say they're in your summer program?"

"Yes, they are. And that's not even the thing so much. It's not a conflict of interest like when Myles was Violet's teacher in the public school. No one cares if I'm dating the father of kids in the daycare."

"Then...?"

"How did Myles handle taking on someone else's kids?" The words exploded out of Alaina. "How did he get over that hurdle? He was so good with Violet today, getting her down out of the tree at the park."

"It's a bit different, I guess. Myles knows Stephan will never come back and question how he's parenting Sam and Violet." Adriana's eyes met Alaina's. "Cameron's ex could show back up."

"There's that, but it's more... I don't know. I don't want to play second fiddle to Evan and Oliver. Does that sound selfish and terrible? I want Cameron to myself like most couples just starting out. But he'll never be mine that way. He'll always be the twins' dad."

Adriana nodded slowly. "Okay, I think I see what you're saying. That was a problem for Myles, too, at first."

"What happened? How did he get over it?"

"Well, everything changed when he saved Violet's life, but I'm sure you'd rather not do something so drastic, and it probably won't ever be called for. But that's how he proved to her that he'd be the kind of dad who'd do anything for his daughter. And that's what finally won Mom and Dad over, too."

Like Alaina was going to seek out a crisis like the one that had melded her sister's family into a unit. No thanks. There had to be a different way — an easier way — to get over this mental hurdle with the twins.

"Have you tried taking the boys out on a date, one at a time? I mean, just you and Oliver then another time with Evan. Not with Cameron."

Alaina levered a stare at her sister. "Are you kidding me?"

"Not in the slightest. If you're thinking about becoming part of their family, you'll need to put in some effort to get to know each boy individually."

"I'm not sure I want to be part of *their* family," she blurted out. "I want a family of my own."

"Then you need to break up with Cameron before things

go much further. It's not fair to him or the twins to lead them on if you have no intention of marrying him."

Alaina chomped down on her lip.

"Because the option you want — Cameron without his sons — doesn't exist. He's a package deal, sis."

∽ℓ℮

"Do you mind putting the boys to bed tomorrow evening? I want to take Alaina into Twin Falls for a concert."

Dad tapped his pencil against the newspaper and looked at Cameron for a long moment before exchanging a glance with Mom. The silence was deafening. "I don't think so, son."

"I didn't know you had plans. I can find a sitter." He'd rarely needed one in the past eighteen months since his sister had moved to Arcadia Valley. It wasn't like he had anywhere to be in the evenings. Not before Alaina.

"Are the boys asleep now?" asked Mom.

Cameron nodded. "Can I fix you a cup of tea?"

Mom rose to her feet. "I'll do it. You sit down. You worked hard today."

"It's not a problem—"

"Let me take care of you."

He shrugged and sat at the kitchen table around the corner from Dad. "So what are you two up to tomorrow then?" They'd gone to Joanna and Grady's a few times, and to Barry and Linda's about once a week. If they were actually forming a friendship with Grady's parents, that might take up more of their time.

134

Wait. His parents were looking at each other again. Doing that silent speak thing.

Dad folded the newspaper with the crossword puzzle on top then laid it on the table. He removed his glasses and placed them on top of the paper. "We don't feel what you are doing is right, Cameron. Your mother and I have talked and prayed about it, and we've come to the conclusion we can't pave your path to this girl."

Was there any chance of keeping every thought and reaction captive? What were the right words to say? Cameron shot up a prayer of his own. "So you are telling me that, because I'm divorced, you've decided to stand in the way of me dating a lovely Christian woman."

The tea kettle's whistle rose, and Mom pulled the kettle off the heat. "Dating is for single people, son."

"I'm single."

Dad shook his head. "Your marriage covenant is broken. You made promises before God and witnesses and then didn't keep them."

Cameron surged to his feet. "I kept them. You know I did. It's Lisa who—"

"You can't blame her for everything."

"I'm *not* blaming her for everything. I wasn't perfect. I'm still not." As his parents were only too happy to remind him of. "But she is the one who had an affair, not me. She's the one who walked out of this house on another man's arm. She's the one who sent divorce papers for me to sign."

Mom tut-tutted. "She was always a wild one."

"And that's not important anymore. Lisa is gone, Mom. She made her choices, and her choices didn't include the boys and me. What would you say if she walked in the door right now? 'Welcome home, honey'?"

"Well, she *is* your wife."

"No, she's not. She *was* my wife. Once we signed divorce papers, we were no longer married. It's over. Lisa isn't coming back and, if she tried, I wouldn't trust her. I'd have no obligation before God to accept her. Before the divorce was finalized? Maybe. But now, not at all."

"Your marriage isn't broken in God's eyes."

He laughed, a sharp bitter sound. "Oh, yes, it is. It's shattered to the point there's nothing left. Don't you understand? Lisa isn't coming back."

Dad cleared his throat. "We're sorry about that, son. Believe me. But it doesn't give you license to go chasing some other young thing in a skirt. We can't make you see reason, it seems, but we can keep our own consciences clean."

Cameron tried to shake off the red spots forming in front of his eyes, tried to swallow the angry words that wanted to pour out. He clenched his hands and unclenched them. Counted to ten. Then fifty.

"Here's your tea, son."

Tea? They shoved holier-than-thou platitudes in front of his face and then offered him chamomile tea? That was almost funny. Although the stuff was supposed to be calming. "Thanks."

Tea sloshed onto the table from his shaking hands. No. He couldn't do this. Couldn't maintain a civil conversation when he was so angry. "I'm going for a run, if it's okay with you." He raised his eyebrows and pinned his glare on his father. "Unless it's against your conscience to stay with the boys for half an hour unless I promise not to go to Alaina's." He managed to tamp most of the sarcasm out of his voice.

Not that he was in any frame of mind to talk to her. She didn't deserve all this dumped on her. Not when she'd been a bit moody herself lately. Huh. Probably her parents were giving her as much grief as his were giving him. Great. Both of them in their late twenties with interfering parents.

"We can sit with the boys for half an hour," Mom announced. "We haven't finished the crossword puzzle in the paper yet. Don't worry. We'll leave the Sudoku for you."

They hadn't — oh, good grief.

Cameron gave a curt nod and strode to his room to change into running shorts and a T-shirt before letting himself out the back door. He couldn't trust himself to speak to them.

He'd save it all up for talking to God as he pounded down the streets of Arcadia Valley. Contrary to what his parents seemed to believe, he did care about hearing God's voice in return.

Chapter 15

J 'M SORRY. I have to cancel for tomorrow night.

Alaina stared at the text message. What was going on? She'd been looking forward to going to the folk concert in Twin Falls for several days. So had Cameron, for that matter.

She tapped a reply. *Is everything okay?*

If you're still up, may I phone?

It might be 10:30, and she'd been reading to unwind before bed. But... if they didn't talk, she wouldn't get much sleep. She'd be too worried. *Okay*, she tapped back.

Two seconds later, her phone rang, and she answered quickly to prevent Kenia from hearing it. Not that it really mattered, she supposed. "Hello?"

"Hi, sweetheart. I wasn't sure if you'd still be awake."

"Just getting ready for bed. What's up?" She held her breath, an onslaught of worry tackling her. Had he decided he didn't want to go out with her anymore, after all?

"It's my parents." He heaved a mighty sigh that echoed through her phone. "You know they're unhappy about me dating. It's not you," he added hurriedly. "It's me. They're convinced that I've had my one shot at marriage, and that I'm disobeying God by even thinking about doing it again."

Alaina had known all along that dating Cameron wasn't as casual as the guys she'd gone out with when she was younger. She could see how a single father didn't invite a woman out unless he was looking at the long-term picture. On the other hand, she was twenty-eight herself, more than ready to settle down. "You've told me this before. Has something new come up?" She tried to imagine his parents with medieval torture devices, turning screws into his thumbnails to force his obedience.

"I asked them if they'd be willing to watch the boys tomorrow night. The answer was no, that they'd talked things over and decided they can no longer encourage my wayward behavior. They like spending time with the boys — most of the time — so it's not that part. It's just they feel like they're encouraging me to sin."

"Maybe you could get a different sitter? Or maybe..." No, she didn't want to offer he could bring the boys along. Not really. She'd never thought of dating as a family affair, and she didn't want to start now.

"I'll make some phone calls tomorrow morning on my coffee break. My usual sitters haven't been needed for a while, but it might be time to start putting them back in the loop."

Alaina wracked brain trying to think of someone who might be able to manage Cameron's boisterous twins. But she'd been out of Arcadia Valley for so long, she no longer had a clue what teenagers were even available. Some of the kids she used to care for probably were watching other people's kids now. "I was really looking forward to this concert." She held her breath, waiting for a reply.

"Me, too." His voice gentled. "Not just the concert. Spending time with you, Alaina. I treasure every bit of time we can spend together."

She dared to breathe. It seemed they were still on the same page. "Is there another night that band will be in Twin Falls?"

"No, it was just a one-off concert. And I only have two tickets. So even if we wanted to take the boys along, I couldn't do that."

Guilt rolled over Alaina as she realized he would've been perfectly willing to bring the twins. Well, maybe not *perfectly* willing, but the question had been moot. Her parents? There was no way they'd be willing to watch the kids, not after the way Mom had made a big deal of wondering if Alaina knew what she was getting in for. The question had annoyed her like crazy.

Of course she knew. Did she look like she had the word 'stupid' stamped across her forehead? "Adriana and Myles left this morning for Spokane, or I could've asked her." A sudden thought struck her. "How about taking the boys out to Evelyn and Ben's? Do you think they'd mind?"

"I can't ask. They have so much going on, and the boys do really poorly at being woken up, buckled into the car, and taken home at midnight. So they'd have to stay overnight, and that's not really an option with either Ben's or Evelyn's work schedules."

So they were back to needing someone who could fill in

at his house. "Did something in particular happen to make your parents change their mind?"

He sighed. "If there was, they didn't say anything to me about it. I asked if they had any plans for tomorrow evening just like I've done many times in the past few weeks, and this time they exchanged *that* look. You know the one. Parents have been perfecting it for millennia."

Alaina forced a chuckle. Had Cameron and Lisa practiced that look as well? Or did it only come after thirty-plus years of a compatible marriage? "Yeah, my parents seem pretty good at that one themselves." Even Adriana and Myles seemed to be figuring it out.

How was this ever going to work with Cameron? She was falling for the guy, hook, line, and sinker, but the logistics were beyond anything she'd ever experienced in her life. It wasn't just him. If it was — even with his divorce with Lisa in his past — she could deal with it, but the twins added so much complexity. Not that they were bad kids, exactly. They had quick minds, especially Evan, and were quite precocious. It was just that they existed at all.

Was it so wrong to want to date a guy who didn't offer a ready-made family? Not that she had any excuse. She'd known from the very first instant she met Cameron that he was the father of two unruly little boys. Why hadn't she steered clear at Joanna and Grady's wedding reception? No, she'd seen something in him even then that proved to be irresistible. She didn't want someone else. At all. Ever. She was in love with Cameron Kraus.

But the boys…

"Alaina?"

"I'm sorry. My brain went off wool gathering. I guess if you don't have a sitter for tomorrow night then we're not going anywhere." She forced a chuckle. "It's pretty simple, really."

"Like I said, I'll make a few phone calls tomorrow on my coffee break and see if I can come up with a plan. But if not, maybe we can do something else. Together with the boys, I mean."

Was this how every date was going to be from here on out? A scramble to find a sitter, or wind up taking the boys along? *Alaina, deal with it. You're this far in, you can't just bail out now.* But couldn't she? Cameron deserved someone who loved not only him but his sons. And even more to the point, the twins deserved someone who truly loved them. A new mom shouldn't only put up with them because she loved their father. That seemed to be the premise behind just about every kids' movie she'd ever seen with a stepmother in it. She couldn't be that woman. But what did it mean?

"I'll be in touch tomorrow, sweetheart. It will all work out. I promise."

"Okay. I look forward to hearing from you in the morning then."

"Sweet dreams." His voice was gentle, soft.

Her heart flipped over in her chest at his tender words. "You, too. Sleep tight."

With the call disconnected, Alaina lay back against her pillows with her hands behind her head.

"God? I'm so confused. My parents aren't all that thrilled about Cameron and the boys, either, but they're much nicer about it than his are. I know the Bible says we are to honor our mothers and fathers, but is there ever an end to that? Does honoring them mean obeying them even when you're twenty-eight years old?"

Could a person honor without obeying?

"Please show me what to do, God. I don't even know. Everything inside me is such a muddle unless I'm spending time with Cameron. Then everything seems right with my world. I know he loves You, and I know he wants Your perfect will for his life. So do I. So that's another way I'm really confused, God. Can You, like, send a lightning strike from heaven or something? Something that will help us know, beyond a shadow of a doubt, what Your will is in this?"

She reached for her Bible, and opened it to Ephesians chapter three. Those verses about being grounded and rooted in God's love. Were they the answer? Sure, she'd been going to church since she moved back to Arcadia Valley. She hadn't even sat beside Cameron, so it wasn't as though he was a distraction to her. But was she going from force of habit, because it was the expectation in her family? Or was she truly trying to seek God's will in everything? That might be the first question she needed to answer.

Frustrated, Cameron leaned back in his office chair. The three girls he had hired occasionally to babysit the twins were all busy this evening. Too bad he hadn't been able to give them any more warning, although the Quintana girl had a part-time job at El Corazon now, so she wouldn't have been available anyway. What was he going to do?

He reached for his phone and tapped his sister's number. It wasn't that he wanted her to babysit, so much, although he wouldn't turn her down. He just needed some perspective on their parents.

"Hey, Cameron!" Her cheery voice came through his phone. "Aren't you at work?"

"It's my coffee break. I'm sitting in my office, trying to line up a babysitter. Do you know anyone who might be available to put the boys to bed and stay with them this evening?"

"Um, our parents are actually going out somewhere?"

Cameron pinched the bridge of his nose. "No, Dad decided they can no longer endorse my evil ways."

Joanna laughed, followed by a short uncomfortable silence. "Wait a minute. You're serious, aren't you?"

"Altogether too much. I'm sure you've heard a thing or two from them about your wayward brother."

"Well, yes. Of course, they've mentioned it a time or two."

Probably two or three times per visit.

"So, something changed? What happened, do you know?"

"No clue. I scored two tickets to a concert in Twin Falls for tonight, but when I mentioned it to them, they gave each other that look — you know the one — and said they could no longer make it easy for me to disobey God."

His sister let out a long sigh. "I guess this doesn't completely surprise me."

"Yeah, me neither. But they've been so willing for the past month that I wasn't prepared for things to change without any warning."

"What are you going to do?"

"Well, I haven't been able to find a sitter, so I guess the concert is out. There are no more seats left so I couldn't take the boys along even if I wanted to. Maybe you'd like the tickets?"

"Thanks, but no. We've had a busy week and need an evening in. Besides, that's not what I meant."

Cameron stared out the window of his office, processing her words. It took a minute to put the pieces together. "You're asking if I'm going to bend to their wishes and break up with Alaina?"

"It does sound kind of absurd. You're twenty-nine."

"Trust me, I'm aware of that. I just don't know... how long is this whole honor your father and mother thing supposed to be good for, anyway? If we follow that all the way to the end result, you'd have sixty-year-olds asking their parents' permission to do just about anything, when their parents are in their eighties."

Joanna chuckled. "Can you just see Grady's dad taking Granddad's advice on something now? He just turned ninety, and you know how his mind is slipping."

"My point exactly."

"Do you want the boys to come to our house and spend the night? Although I'm not sure I want to get in the middle of what's going on with Mom and Dad."

"I'm not really asking that. Besides, you already said you needed a peaceful evening at home. But, as far as I'm concerned, the question is much greater, and I don't even know where to begin looking for the answers. I guess the biggest one is, do you really think... no, I know you don't."

"Do I really think what, Cameron?"

"You've encouraged me to get into the dating game again. So I assume you don't think that I've had my one chance at marital happiness, and that ship has sailed, never to return to my port again."

"You're right. Somehow our parents didn't manage to instill that whole belief system in me. I guess I never had to consider the ramifications personally, because neither Grady nor I have ever been married before. Although, I know a lot of people who think the church has gone way too far in saying it doesn't matter what sin anyone has committed. After all, God is a loving God, and He'll forgive you no matter what."

Joanna, too? Cameron shook his head and pulled to his feet. He walked over to his window and stared into the busy potato-chip plant below him. "I don't even know what to say to that, sis. It's like God has quit the business of forgiving people."

"I wish I had a quick answer for you, Cameron. I wish I could point to Joanna 1:1 with the authority of Scripture and just make it clear that divorce isn't the only terrible thing that can happen to anyone. I know you have many regrets. You've told me you know you could've been a better husband to Lisa."

Cameron bit his lip, stifling the urge to defend himself, but she spoke truth. He might not have been the one who had an affair. He might not have been the one who left, but that didn't mean he was blameless in the whole thing. He was only human, after all.

"Somehow this reminds me of some of the questions Jesus was asked when he was on earth," Joanna went on. "You know, the ones where the Pharisees tried to trip him up by asking a question where either answer was going to get him into trouble with someone."

"Your point?"

"My point is that Jesus often gave a totally unexpected answer. Remember the woman who was brought to him having been caught in adultery?"

A small amount of hope began to bubble up in Cameron soul. "Yes?"

"Even though the penalty prescribed by the law was pretty clear, Jesus didn't say to them, 'You're right. You all should start stoning her right now.'"

Cameron leaned his back against the window and closed his eyes. "No, He said the one without sin should cast the first stone. He knew all of them had done something wrong."

"Exactly! He rendered all those Pharisees speechless. They still knew they were right, but they also knew there wasn't any way to argue with what Jesus had just said."

"So there is an answer somewhere."

"I think there is, bro. Grady and I will be praying for you and Alaina. And for Mom and Dad, for that matter. So, back to the earlier question? Do you want to bring the boys over tonight?"

Cameron thought it over for just a minute. "No, you're right. The most important thing right now is to be praying and seeking for that third answer. Not the judgmental 'no' or the easy-going 'yes,' but something else." He rubbed his forehead, where a headache was threatening to ruin the rest of the day. He let out a sardonic chuckle. "Now, if I only had any clue what that third answer might be."

Chapter 16

ALAINA HADN'T LAUGHED so hard in a long time. Evan and Oliver were genuinely funny when there weren't a bunch of other kids around, something she'd never had a chance to notice at the summer program. The four of them had sat around Cameron's kitchen table with *Sushi Go,* the game Joanna had brought back from their honeymoon for the twins. The boys were hilarious as they tried to collect more portions of a Japanese meal than the other one did. Competitive little monkeys.

Cameron's eyes met hers across the table, and he grinned, the crinkles around his eyes deepening. Why had she spent so long dreading time alone with Cameron and the boys? She knew. She wanted to be romanced. Maybe she was a little bit selfish. Everything wasn't always all about her. Not when Cameron could look at her that way.

Had Garth ever...? Not really. She didn't even want to go there.

"Okay, boys. That was the last round, and now you're off to bed."

"But I don't want to," whined Evan.

Oliver, on the other hand, looked at Alaina through questioning eyes. "Will you read us a bedtime story?"

Her gaze snapped to Cameron's and then back to his son's. Oh, boy. But how could she turn the little guy down? He looked at her with such a hopeful expression on his face. "Yes, I'm sure I could do that. What kind of stories are you reading with your dad these days?"

Oliver's shoulders shrugged dramatically. "Whatever he wants to, usually."

Alaina raised her eyebrows at Cameron. "While I'm impressed that you're reading bedtime stories to the boys, aren't you into a series or something with them yet?"

He shook his head with a rueful grin. "I don't even know where to start, to be honest."

"Well, I'll see what I can find tonight. But then I think I'll ask my sister what kinds of books Sam and Violet liked when they were the boys' age."

"Reading is for sissies," declared Evan.

Alaina kept a firm smile. "That's where you're wrong, young man. Stories can take you anywhere in the world you want to go."

He looked at her with raised eyebrows, disbelief evident on his young face.

"I'm not kidding. Not only can you go any place, but you can go to any time, as well. Like any era in history. Or..." She lowered her voice mysteriously. "Or to places in the future. And, not only that, stories can take you places that exist only in your imaginations."

Oliver and Evan exchanged a look. "Are you pulling our

leg?" asked Evan.

"Not at all." She looked over at Cameron. "Are you a reader?"

He lifted a shoulder with an apologetic shrug. "I used to be, years ago. I sort of lost the habit, I guess."

"Well, there's no excuse for that. E-readers have been invented, and there are so many choices available these days you just wouldn't believe it. Everyone needs a hobby."

"I do Sudoku."

She rolled her eyes. "That doesn't count. Math is boring. What kind of books did you like to read back when you still did?"

"Science fiction." His eyes gleamed. "Science is applied math, you know."

Shaking her head, Alaina turned to the twins. "Do you know what science fiction is?"

Both boys shook their heads, looking between her and their dad as though the adults were speaking a foreign language.

"It's what I was just telling you about, when you can read stories that take place in the future. I know you boys like space, because we've talked about the solar system at daycare. Well, there are stories about people in the future who travel from one planet to the other in spaceships and have adventures."

Oliver's eyes grew around. "Are they true stories?"

Alaina leaned closer to him. "They're not true stories *yet*," she said in a conspiratorial whisper. "But some day, they might be."

"I want that kind of story," said Evan.

151

"I'll ask Sam what kind of science fiction stories he thinks you two would like. Or we can check in at the library and ask Mrs. Delis sometime. But for now, it's time to get things cleaned up here and get you boys off to bed."

That would leave her and Cameron alone in his house for the first time. The concert would've been a lot of fun. She was sure of it. It was a band she'd wanted to see in person ever since she first heard their songs on Spotify a year or two ago. But it was not to be and, while this seemed like a poor substitution at first, they'd had a really good time.

"Off you two go, then," said Cameron. "Get into your pajamas and brush your teeth, okay?"

"But, Dad..." whined Evan.

"You've already had a snack, and it's past your bedtime. Just go do it."

The two boys slouched out of the room, looking as desolate as if their beloved puppy had died.

Alaina stifled a giggle as she looked across the table at Cameron. He reached for her hands, and she clasped his. His thumb rubbed circles on the backs of her hands, causing a thrill to run through her.

"Don't be too long," he whispered, his voice full of promise. "I'll just get the boys ready for bed — ready for your story, I mean — and then clean up here while you're tucking them in."

Down the hallway, she could hear water running and the scrubbing sound of a toothbrush. Such domestic sounds, ones she hadn't known she ever wanted to hear.

She rose to her feet, rounded the table, and stopped behind his chair. He leaned back against her as she rubbed his shoulders gently with strong thumbs. "Thank you, Cameron. I was disappointed about the concert, but this turned out to be pretty fun after all."

He tipped his head back so she could see his eyes, those deep, dark, coffee-colored eyes. "The evening's not over yet, sweetheart."

She bent to kiss his forehead just as the boys called from their bedroom.

That was the sort of promise she could get behind.

Cameron loaded the dishwasher with the plates and cutlery from their Greek take-out. Down the hallway, he heard Alaina's lilting voice as she read something to the boys that he didn't recognize. Maybe she'd found the old set of children's encyclopedias he'd kept from his own childhood. In just a few minutes, she'd be back in the living room with him, and they'd find something to watch on Netflix. Or, maybe, there would just be a lot of snuggling and kissing. He could live with that, too.

He pulled the living room drapes and dimmed the lights. Did he have any candles around? Only if Lisa had left any. Never mind. He didn't want mood lighting that badly.

Thumping sounded from the basement stairwell. Cameron turned, frowning. As far as he knew, his parents had been staying in this evening. They'd claimed they didn't have any other plans, but they weren't willing to babysit the boys so he and Alaina could go out. Fine. Alaina had been right.

They'd had a terrific date right here at the house with both boys.

The footsteps grew louder. A rap sounded at the door that separated the two units, and then the door opened, and his parents strolled in. Dad looked a little sheepish, as though this were not entirely his idea, but Mom had pursed lips and a determined set to her jaw.

Cameron's stomach fell. He didn't even need to make any guesses to know why they showed up on his doorstep. Not when they knew the boys went to bed at eight o'clock. He crossed his arms and leaned back against the kitchen counter. "Anything I can do for you?"

Mom looked around, like she could spot Alaina hiding in a cupboard. "Is she here?"

"Depends on who you mean by she." Cameron kept his voice even, though it was all he could do.

Mom narrowed her gaze at him. "As though you don't know who I'm talking about. Her car is parked right outside."

"Oh, you're asking about Alaina Silva? She does have a name, you know." Cameron straightened and took a step closer to his mother. "May I ask what you're doing here right now?"

Mom shot a glance over her shoulder at Dad, but he was focused on the floor. "We're worried about you, son. We feel it's a bad idea for you to entertain her here in your house with the children asleep."

"I expected this out of you when I was a teenager, Mom, but I'm twenty-nine. I'm an adult, and this is my house. You and Dad are staying in my basement suite as guests, not as anyone who has authority over me. If you're worried that

Alaina and I are going to have sex—"

His mother winced and brought her hand up to cover her chest.

"Sex. It's a word. And it's something that I won't do again until I'm married." He pointed at the door still ajar behind his father. "Now, if you don't mind, I'm sure you have things you'd like to do downstairs. Maybe there's a jigsaw or crossword puzzle calling your name. Or maybe a commentary on the book of Ezra. Either way, I didn't invite you here, and I would like you to go."

Mom's eyes widened, and it occurred to Cameron that her gaze landed somewhere past his arm. He turned and caught sight of Alaina standing in the doorway to the living room, a stormy expression on her face.

He held out his hand toward her, but she only wrapped her arms around her middle and stayed right where she was, her gaze pinned on his mother.

"Is that really all you think of us?" Alaina's voice strengthened with each word.

Now he recognized the storminess. Anger. For sure.

She took a step closer. "So, you'd like to visit with us? Play a game? Watch a movie? You're here because you'd like to get to know me better?"

Mom's gaze flickered but held.

"Or because you think we need a chaperone? We don't, I promise you."

"Maybe you do. What will the neighbors think, seeing your car parked out front until all hours?"

"All hours? It isn't even eight-thirty!"

Enough already. Cameron slid his arm around Alaina's

waist, not that she melted against him. "Mom, who cares what the neighbors think? The Espinozas live across the street. Felipe knows me well enough not to believe the worst of me with no reason." Unlike his own mother. "Old Mr. Taylor lives next door. He sits on his back porch, smiling while he watches the boys play, remembering when his kids were young. He's not jumping to conclusions."

Mom scowled. "You should avoid even giving a hint of immorality."

He raised his eyebrows. "Besides, all my neighbors know my parents are living in my basement. I'm pretty sure that saves my reputation right there." At least, if any of his neighbors had chatted with either Mom or Dad over the fence.

"Well, I've said my piece." Mom huffed.

Dad stood behind her, still examining the floor.

A surge of impatience for both of them washed over Cameron. *Lord, is it too much to ask for them to leave for England tomorrow? Or for somewhere else? Anywhere?*

Was that really what he wanted? He took a deep breath. No, what he really wanted was for them to stop judging and trust him. To treat him like an adult and, perhaps, a friend.

Like that would ever happen.

Dad tugged Mom's arm and turned to the stairs. He hadn't even said a word.

Mom sent one more shot. "God is always watching you."

"I know. And He knows we have nothing to hide."

With a final glare at them both, Mom shut the door behind them with a firm click.

If Cameron expected Alaina to lean against him in relief,

he'd missed the mark.

She pulled away from him. "Where does she get off on that kind of attitude?"

"I don't know." He watched Alaina stalk across the kitchen. "She's always been a bit like this, but she's been really pushy lately, even for her."

"My blood is boiling, I'm so angry."

Cameron nodded. He got it. His own blood pressure was only just starting to subside. One thing was certain, if all Mom wanted to do was douse the mood, she'd succeeded.

Chapter 17

ALAINA SHOOK HER HEAD at her roommate. "I can't join you on your girls' night in. I don't know Evelyn and Joanna as well as you do, and spending time with Joanna right now just seems weird."

"What would you say if I told you my sister-in-law specifically asked for you?"

Alaina forced a chuckle. "That's even more frightening."

Kenia punched her shoulder lightly. "There's nothing scary about Joanna."

"You're not the one dating her brother." Although after that scene with his parents the other night, things had been a little awkward with her and Cameron, anyway. Why did they have to be so judgmental? Why couldn't they open their minds to Cameron finding happiness once again? Not things she wanted to talk to Kenia about, but having a heart-to-heart with Joanna was also not in her cards.

Kenia batted her eyelashes. "Come on. You know you want to. Besides, we're having the party right here at the cottage on Saturday night. So if you don't want to participate, you'll want to stay somewhere else. Maybe with your parents?" Kenia's eyebrows rose.

As if. Cameron's parents might be the most vocal, but it wasn't as though Alaina had given her parents a chance to say anything lately. They had strong opinions, too, but Alaina was pretty sure they'd come around if she just sat down and explained to them how much she loved Cameron. Maybe she should do that.

But therein lay the problem. Did she love him enough? Sure, he kept reminding her that his parents were heading back to England in just a few weeks. But even with an ocean separating them, was there any way she could be their daughter-in-law and live to tell the tale?

She heaved a sigh. "I reserve the right to go in my room and shut the door if things become unpleasant."

"I have no idea why you think that might happen." Kenia angled her head and gave her a knowing look. "Is there something you haven't told me?"

Alaina tried for a bright, sunny smile. "Oh, honey. There's so much I haven't told you, you just wouldn't believe it."

Kenia laughed. "Now that's the spirit."

"They're spending the night? Aren't they both, like, newlyweds?"

Kenia shrugged. "Not for the whole night. But they might

not go home until well after midnight. I've got snacks and games and movies planned. And I really want you to stay for it."

Alaina held up both hands. "Fine, I'll stay."

She wondered what she'd gotten herself into the next evening as the four of them settled around the coffee table playing Blackout. She was so terrible at this sort of game, trying to guess the odds and have them work in her favor. That might even be some sort of metaphor for life. What were the odds she would fall in love with a divorced man? She shook her head.

"So how are things going with my baby brother?" Joanna slapped a four of diamonds onto the table and glanced over at Alaina.

Did she have to answer that? Alaina made a show of picking through the cards in her hands. "Okay."

"Don't let my parents run your life, Alaina. They mean well, but they're so hidebound, it's impossible for them to see past the end of their noses."

Alaina played her card and turned to Evelyn. "Your turn."

"What I'm trying to say is, if you truly love Cameron and he loves you, and you've both prayed about it, then don't let them stand in your way."

"Easy for you to say. You have Barry and Linda for in-laws. What's not to like about them?"

Kenia and Joanna looked at each other and gave each other a high five as they chuckled.

Okay, Alaina was missing something, which wouldn't be the first time. Whatever.

"You don't know the half of it. Linda was pretty sure I was after Grady just because the family has money. Our first few meetings were beyond awkward."

"I remember you hiding in the powder room the first time you came for Sunday dinner." Kenia shook her head, her eyes gleaming. "It took a while for them to realize that you weren't like Grady's old girlfriend, Vanessa."

"I know, right? Just like Granddad kept asking if I was Vanity. How did the poor girl ever get that nickname anyway?"

Kenia shrugged as she turned back to Alaina. "Just saying not everyone gets off to the best start with the future in-laws."

"Isn't that the truth," put in Evelyn. "Ben's dad is an alcoholic, and he barely remembers Maisie and me from one time to the next. It seems his memory is shot worse than Granddad Akers."

Alaina had heard a bit of Evelyn and Ben's story. "But you knew his mom for years before you ever met Ben, right? And loved her."

"It's true. But that was during the years she was estranged from her family. Let's just put it this way, Alaina. When we were kids, we probably thought everyone else had the perfect family, even if we knew we didn't. But then when we grew up — and some of us grew up more abruptly than others — we discovered that just because someone has become an adult doesn't mean they don't have hang-ups and prejudices affecting them every day."

Right, Evelyn's parents had kicked her out when she told them she was pregnant with Maisie in the fall of her junior year of high school. At least Alaina hadn't had to spring *that* on her parents.

"Just remember you're marrying the man, not his family." Kenia slapped her final card on the table. "I think I win this round."

"That's where you're wrong," said Evelyn.

Kenia looked up in surprise. "Did you have more points than me?"

"No, silly. That's not what I meant. You do marry each other's families. How a man was raised and his relationship with his parents and siblings affects everything he does and says for the rest of his life. It's impossible to divorce the two." She grimaced. "Sorry for using that word."

Alaina felt Joanna's eyes watching her. "Is it time for popcorn and a movie yet? I don't really want to talk about this."

Joanna's hand covered Alaina's. "I don't want to make you uncomfortable. I do want you to know that I like you, and my brother obviously adores you. Even the twins keep talking about Miss Alaina." She winked. "And it's not all from the goings-on at the Grace summer program either."

Kenia rotated her shoulders then gathered up the cards. "Hey, did you guys hear that Serena VanderMay, the actress who starred in those teenage ninja movies, has been living incognito in Arcadia Valley for the past two years? You've probably seen her pottery around town. She goes by Serena Johnson now."

Evelyn nodded. "Yes, I was working at the greenhouse gardens one evening back in June when a photographer came and took pictures of her as she helped weed the gardens. She was with Micah Baxter."

Kenia's eyes grew round. "Seriously? You've known all along, and you never told me?"

"How was I to know it would make any difference to you? They *are* dating, you know. Her and Micah."

Kenia clutched her hand over her heart and leaned back dramatically. "How come other women always get the great guys? How come everyone in Arcadia Valley is falling in love except for me?"

Evelyn grinned. "Well, there is still one Baxter brother left. Have you met Jonah?"

"He's adorable." Kenia sighed. "But he'd never notice me."

"Have you ever seen him around Gloria Sinclair?" put in Joanna. "I think he's hoping for something there."

Evelyn shook her head. "Felipe says they're only friends. So Kenia might still have a chance."

Felipe Espinoza was a good friend of Ben's, and he worked on the police force with Gloria Sinclair. Alaina figured he ought to know.

"Nope," said Joanna. "Not to downplay Kenia's feminine charms, but I bet you dollars to donuts Jonah and Gloria will get together sometime." Her eyes twinkled as she looked at Alaina. "At least, I'd bet that if I hadn't been taught that gambling was a mortal sin."

Cameron rested his elbows on the table at the Sunrise Café and looked around the table at his guy friends. At least his parents hadn't stopped watching the boys on Saturday mornings so Cameron could attend the church men's group. They usually had a hearty breakfast in the back room of the Sunrise, while sharing how the Lord was working in their hearts and praying for each other. "So, I have a question for you."

Eight sets of expectant eyes focused on him, including his brother-in-law's.

"This whole 'honor your mother and father' thing that's in the Bible. How far do we take it? When parents give well-meaning but misguided advice to their son who is nearly thirty, how much weight should that son give to their advice?"

"That can be a tough one," said Corban DeWitt. "Although my parents have been gone for several years now, I always believed they had my best interest at heart when they would sit me down to talk something over."

"My situation is probably different as well," said Grady. "A lot of my relationship with my parents these days is on the business end, as we prepare for Dad to hand over the reins of Akers Garden Center to me."

Did no one else at the table have interfering parents? Cameron's gaze slid across the Baxter brothers. Their parents were dead and gone as well. He looked over at Ben.

Ben lifted both hands. "My dad is an alcoholic, and being as the only advice he ever gave me was to go find some girl to have sex with or to have another drink, I think the line was pretty easy for me to find. I mean, so much of his advice was contrary to Scripture."

Cameron let out a long slow breath. Would these guys have his back if he bared his soul to them? Or would they side with his parents and denounce him for even thinking of remarrying? He shot a glance at his brother-in-law. Surely Grady and Joanna had talked the situation over. Cameron couldn't imagine why they wouldn't have. And wasn't Grady's opinion worth more than all the other guys in the room put together? Maybe he should pull Grady aside rather than get into everything with the group.

"What's on your mind?" asked Corban.

Too late to go private.

Cameron didn't miss the fact that Malachi Baxter's brother, Micah, signed half the discussion to his deaf twin. Sometime he should find out about the bond between Micah and Malachi. How close would Evan and Oliver be when they grew up? But that wasn't the question on the table now. He looked around the group again. Was his reluctance simply because he didn't want to find out that everyone else would give him the same advice his parents had? But it wasn't the same direction that his own thoughts went after praying. How many hours had he spent with his head between his hands, asking God for wisdom?

"Okay, here goes. You all know that I've been divorced. The twins' mother left us about three years ago. Ran off with my best friend. Needless to say, Kyle and I aren't really on speaking terms anymore, even though Lisa left him only a few months later."

Why was he starting back there? Surely all these guys knew his history. He placed his hands on the table. "So, I've met someone. Some of you probably already know that. The

Bible doesn't have very encouraging things to say about adultery, divorce, and remarriage. My parents believe that I've had my one and only chance at being married. But, although I have spent a lot of time in prayer, I can't hear God telling me the same thing. I know it's not a committee decision." He forced out a chuckle. "But I would appreciate two things from you men. I consider you all my friends. I'd like to ask you to pray for Alaina Silva and me as we navigate the situation."

Grady snickered. *"Navigate the situation?* I thought you said you were in love."

Grady's words lightened the atmosphere a little. Cameron looked around at the other guys. "I met her at Joanna and Grady's wedding over a month ago. Her parents own the golf course and country club, and she grew up in Arcadia Valley. Evelyn hired her as the coordinator for the preschool and daycare center at the greenhouses. Because Evan and Oliver are in the summer program there, we see her every day." He held up both hands. "And yes, I'll admit to many an evening out as well."

At the other end of the table, Micah's fingers flicked as he signed what Cameron had said to Malachi.

Corban leaned closer. "So the two things you are asking for are prayer and advice?"

Cameron nodded. Was he really ready to hear if everyone thought he was in the wrong? *Please, Lord, I want to do Your will more than anything else.*

Chapter 18

A LAINA HAD LIVED through girls' night at the cottage. She wouldn't admit it to Kenia, but she'd even had fun. While Joanna had certainly addressed the elephant in the room — if one could call Cameron that — they'd laughed and told jokes and poked fun at Kenia for the rapture in her eyes when she kept gushing about how Serena VanderMay was now signed to do a new movie, one that had reportedly been written with the flat-out intention of luring the star back to Hollywood.

Hollywood hadn't counted on Micah Baxter, though. The whole town was rooting for him, fingers crossed that he and Serena would stay together and that they'd spend at least part of every year in Arcadia Valley.

Alaina parked at the curb of her parents' house. She'd been avoiding them. She knew it, and she was sure they knew it, too. It was time to have a heart-to-heart with them. She'd talked to Adriana on the phone again earlier this morning, and her sister had prayed with her and encouraged her. What would she ever do without Adriana?

Alaina pulled the keys out of the ignition, climbed out of the car, and headed up the walk. It came as no surprise that the front door flew open before she ever got there, her mom standing framed in the doorway, holding out her hands. "Alaina. We've missed you so. Your father is making breakfast. Your favorite, that Tex-Mex zucchini skillet you like so much."

Alaina climbed the steps and pressed her lips against her mother's cheek. "Thanks, Mom." She wasn't all that hungry. Probably because she was a basket of nerves. Her parents would understand that part soon enough.

"How's my favorite baby daughter?" Dad stirred the mass in the cast iron frying pan and turned toward her.

"Doing okay, Dad." She pushed out a small smile.

"Have a seat, darling. Let me pour you a coffee." Mom pulled a mug out of the cupboard and filled it as Alaina took the offered chair.

Mom poured a splash of cream into the coffee and set it in front of Alaina before taking the seat around the corner from her. "How is your new job coming along? All my friends who have grandchildren in the program are very happy with it."

"That's good to hear." Alaina took a sip of the coffee. "Cheri and Whitney are terrific with the children, and we have several part-time staff as well. Considering this is a pilot program, I think it's going very well. Evelyn Kujak is terrific, always ready to help out if there's a logistics problem."

"That's great to hear. She seems a lovely young woman. I understand she is a staunch Christian and has overcome many trials in her past."

Dad began cracking eggs into the skillet on the stove.

Alaina pulled her gaze back to her mom. "Yes. I've met her a few times outside of work as well. She's a friend of my roommate, Kenia." She took a deep breath. "And of Cameron's sister, Joanna, too."

Her parents exchanged glances. "Are you still seeing him?" asked Mom, her voice sounding a little pinched.

"Yes. I wanted to talk to you about Cameron and the boys. That's why I came."

"Oh?" Dad turned from the stove.

"You're happy for Evelyn, and are thrilled that she's walking with Jesus even after having a child out of wedlock." Even that term sounded strange to Alaina's ears, but it was one she'd heard her parents use in the past. "Years ago, a woman who'd found herself pregnant without a husband was pretty much an outcast from society. And yet the church welcomed her in — even giving her a job — and celebrated her marriage to Ben."

Alaina took another sip of her coffee and waited for her parents to process her words. Dad scraped the contents of his cast-iron skillet onto three plates and set them on the table. He reached for Mom's hand and then Alaina's, and the three of them made a circle while he asked the blessing over their meal.

Silence stretched while Dad ate several bites of his breakfast before leaning back in his chair and pinning Alaina with his gaze. "I see were this is going, Alaina, and you're right, to a point, anyway. Many people in the church no longer regard divorce as the most terrible thing in the world, just as they don't denounce each unwed mother."

Mom slid her hand over Dad's, squeezed it, then took up the thread. "You know we'd rather see you fall in love with a young man without this kind of history. We remember the story and the scandal Cameron's wife leaving him caused a few years back. We've also seen how he's humbled himself before the Lord, how he and his sons are in church nearly every week, and believe he is trying to walk with Jesus."

Alaina let out a long breath.

"So, yes, it's a bit of a concern," Dad put in. "But just as much to the point is the fact of those boys. I can't imagine starting off life together with two rambunctious children like them."

"I know. I'll be honest, the twins are my biggest concern as well. Them and the fact that Cameron's parents don't think he should remarry."

Mom's eyebrows rose. "It's not like it's any business of theirs."

Alaina laughed. "Aren't you the ones who had such strong opinions at Christmas time about Adriana and Myles?"

It seemed like a long time since Cameron had been able to take Alaina out for a nice dinner, just the two of them. In the weeks since his parents had burst into the kitchen, all but calling them names, things had hit a bit of a standstill. Cameron wasn't sure how to handle that. It was still three weeks before his parents left for England again, but the fact remained that he wasn't completely comfortable with going against their expressed opinion. He'd been brought up to obey, no matter what, and the habit was deeply ingrained. And yet, when he thought of what they were asking him — no, telling him — to do, it just didn't line up with Scripture, from what he could figure.

"Penny for your thoughts?" Alaina nudged his arm as they walked through Arcadia Creek Park.

He tightened his fingers around hers. "I'm sorry. They're definitely not worth one copper cent. I shouldn't be worrying over things when we finally have a couple of hours to ourselves."

"It was good of Evelyn and Ben to offer to watch the boys for a while," she said.

"Yes." He looked down at Alaina. Maybe his parents were right. Alaina was all that was good and beautiful and right in the world. He didn't deserve her. He didn't deserve a second chance.

She let go of his hand and slipped her arm around his waist.

Cameron could certainly get into that. He copied her action, but it wasn't enough. He turned and drew her into both his arms. "Alaina, I've missed you so much."

She tilted her face toward his, and he pressed a kiss to those inviting lips. Then he caught the excitement in her eyes. "What's up? You look like the cat that swallowed a canary." He could do some good news about now.

"I had a heart-to-heart with my mom and dad a few days ago."

She'd mentioned nothing in the texts they'd exchanged. "Tell me more."

171

"You know they weren't all that excited about us dating, especially at first."

It seemed to be the story of their relationship. "Go on."

"But I think they've come to realize that what we share isn't a passing infatuation." Her eyes searched his. "It's not, is it?"

Cameron's arms tightened around her back. One hand encompassed her waist, while the other tangled in the springy curls across her shoulders. He bent the few inches between them and kissed her thoroughly. When he needed air, he rested his forehead against hers and look deeply into her eyes. "I hope that answers your question. I don't go around kissing casual friends this way."

"I sure hope not." Something dashed across her face like a small cloud, but it was gone as quickly as it had appeared.

Of course she was thinking of Lisa. She'd been the only other woman in his life. But he wasn't sure he'd ever loved her... not this way. It had been easy come and, apparently, easy go. Lots of good times, sure, but at what price? He certainly hadn't been walking close to the Lord during those years.

He slipped his lips across hers and felt a shudder ran through her. One he could certainly feel himself. "Tell me what they said now."

"They still have a few reservations, mostly about the boys, frankly. But they give us their blessing."

Cameron searched her gorgeous brown eyes. His heart began to lift like a hot air balloon beginning to fill. "Really? I'm so thankful."

"Me, too. They did say they'd be willing to spend some

time with the boys themselves." She looked down, a slight blush pinking her cheeks. "At least, they know they need to get to know the boys someday, if we are staying together." She didn't quite meet his eyes.

Cameron tipped her face toward his, one finger under her chin. "Do you want us to?"

Her gaze flicked to his then away, as the flush in her cheeks deepened.

"Alaina, I'm not dating you casually, as a way to get back into the game. Until six weeks ago, I had no intention of ever falling in love again. But then I met you."

This time her eyes remained focused on his, searching him, and her lips parted slightly.

He couldn't resist that invitation but lowered his head and captured her mouth with his. Controlled the kiss, making sure she understood that this wasn't a passing fancy. He wasn't in a light, bubbly, fun little thing called love. No, it was the real thing.

Her response ignited a glow in a fire throughout his body, and he held her close, even as she clutched him. He couldn't have moved away from her, even if he wanted to, but he didn't.

"I love you, Alaina. Don't ever forget. Whatever comes, whatever goes, this is one thing I know is true."

"What about your parents?" She whispered.

"They'll come around. I don't know how, but I know they will." Now that he'd spoken the certainty out loud, he felt it reverberate through him. "This is what I'm praying for in faith, believing." He held her face between both his hands, and brushed his lips over her forehead. "It's what my men's group is praying for, too."

She pulled back a little bit and searched his eyes. "Your men's group is privy to our relationship?"

He wasn't sure exactly what her thoughts were on the subject. Sometimes she was so hard to read. So he just nodded.

Her lips pursed slightly, and it didn't seem to be an invitation for a kiss. Had he done something wrong? He couldn't think how. His thumbs caressed her cheekbones as his fingers gloried in the sensation of her curls against them at the back of her head. "Oh, come on now. Don't tell me you haven't talked to your girlfriends about us."

"Only because they made me. And only a few."

"Alaina? These guys are my best friends. We have a no-gossip policy. Prayers only. I trust them like I trust you."

By the hesitant look in her brown eyes, maybe he should've mentioned this to her before. But he'd stand by his words. How would he ever have gotten through the last three years if it hadn't been for guys like Grady and Corban? Sure, some of the others were more recent additions to their group, like Ben and the Baxter brothers. But they'd formed a strong, tight bond in the year and a half since he'd known them.

"I just hate the thought of everyone talking about us behind our backs."

"No worries, sweetheart. They are there for us."

Chapter 19

I CAN'T BELIEVE HE TOLD all his guy friends about us and what his parents think about it all." Headset in place, Alaina stuffed her cell phone in her pocket as she strode down the block, talking to her sister.

"Isn't it a good thing he has a support network?"

Alaina huffed. "I suppose so, but it's just the fact that he didn't ask me about it."

"Did you tell him you were going to go straight home and call your sister?"

"Of course not."

"Then…" Adriana let the word linger on the airwaves.

Alaina shook her head, not that her sister could see. "It's different. There's like ten guys in that group. They can't all be his best friend. I feel like everyone in town is probably talking about us right now."

"I'm not sure what the problem is." Adriana's voice held firm. "Myles didn't know a soul in Bridgeview when we began dating. He didn't have any sort of network at all. He isn't close to his two brothers and, besides, they aren't believers. I'm thankful he's gotten to know some of the other men in our neighborhood and church since then, but it sure would've been a big help to him to have a group of men who had his back when we first met."

Alaina huffed out a breath. "You're supposed to be on my side."

Her sister laughed. "If that's all you want, you might as well get a parrot. I thought you actually wanted some advice."

"I'm so confused, Adriana. I love him so much. That's not even a question. But I guess... I'm afraid."

"I was just thinking that," said Adriana. "So let's dig into that, shall we? What are you afraid of?"

"You've been hanging around your psychology major friend too much lately." Alaina tried for a casual chuckle, but it didn't quite come out the way she expected it to.

Adriana laughed. "Well, Rebekah has been a big help to both Violet and me as we worked through things in the past six months or so. I'm beginning to think I should have gotten a psychology degree myself."

"It's not too late yet." Alaina couldn't keep the bitterness out of her voice. "Just go ahead and practice on me."

There was a slight pause. Then Adriana said, "You told me Mom and Dad are on board with you dating Cameron. That they'd like to get to know Evan and Oliver. It just doesn't seem like you to be so worried about your boyfriend having a group of strong Christian men as friends. So, is there something even deeper going on?"

"Well, you know that Cameron's parents are dead set against us."

"So you've said, but it hasn't stopped you yet."

Alaina thought about that. "I know."

"So the first thing that comes to mind is that you're hoping, somewhere deep inside, that he will choose to agree with his parents—"

"That's ridiculous!" The words shot out of Alaina's mouth.

"Hear me out, sis. It seems like it was kind of fun for you to date someone who was clearly unsuitable, both from our parents' point of view, and his. You dated a few bad boys back in high school, too."

Alaina chomped down on her lip.

That didn't stop Adriana, though. "And then there was Garth. I think he felt a bit dangerous to you, as well. I know you thought he would pop the question sometime soon, but did you really want him to?"

"I don't even know what you're talking about, Adriana."

"Don't you?"

Did she? Had there been warning signs she'd been ignoring with Garth? Had she been looking for a reason to keep their relationship the way it was, not wanting to commit?

"You're twenty-eight years old, sis."

"I know that," Alaina all but snapped.

"So, now you've found a man who's a strong believer. One who adores you as much as you adore him, from what I could tell over the Fourth of July. You have a chance to grasp happiness with both hands and hang on for the ride. And I don't think it's the fact that his parents are against it, or that he is part of a strong men's group, that's holding you back. So... what is?"

Her sister made way too much sense sometimes. Alaina's eyes burned as she strode down the block, oblivious to traffic going by even on this quiet residential street. "I don't know," she whispered.

Adriana's voice was soft. "But there is something."

"There must be, but I don't know what. Happiness just seems so fleeting sometimes. You and Stephan were so in love, and then he died in that horrible fire. I thought I loved Garth with everything in me, then found out that he was cheating on me. Cameron's been married before, so he obviously thought he'd found his forever love. And he's divorced." Alaina let out a frustrated chuckle. "How does anyone even know if they found a love that lasts?"

"Our parents have done pretty well for the last almost forty years," Adriana offered.

"They have, but Cameron's parents have been married about that long, and I sure wouldn't want a relationship like theirs. His dad is so mousy, just following along and nodding his head at whatever Nora says."

"Do you think that's how Cameron is, too? That he'll let you make all the decisions and just follow along like a well-trained puppy?"

For the life of her, Alaina couldn't imagine it. Cameron had taken charge of their relationship from the beginning, proving to her that he cared about her, which later deepened into love. He'd shown her he could be a good dad as well, even though he seemed to have a predilection for takeout and hadn't moved his kids up to books suitable for their age range. But those were hardly fatal flaws.

"I have to go, sis. But I promise you that Myles and I will

be praying for you. Keep in touch, okay?"

Now why didn't it bother her to know there were people praying for her? Why were Cameron's friends the problem?

She bowed her head as she walked along. *I'm sorry, Lord. Please let me trust You to give good gifts to Your children.*

"You have got to be kidding me." Cameron's mom stared at him in horror. "That's not a suitable excursion for boys who are just turning seven. Why don't you take them to the petting zoo or something? Isn't there that farm where they and their friends can ride a pony for a little while?"

Cameron held his grin in place. "The boys have been to Bigby Farm quite a few times, but they've been begging to ride the zip line ever since Joanna and Grady did it last summer. Even though they thought it was totally yucky that Uncle Grady proposed to Aunt Jonah on the zip line."

His mom cast a fleeting glance at Dad. "Wilfred, tell your son—"

"Nope. My mind is made up. I've told the boys, and they are super excited. I even have reservations made. The only thing I need to know is how many people are going." He raised his eyebrows at his father.

Dad glanced at Mom, as though seeking her permission even to agree with her.

Cameron tilted his head and looked between them. Had this always been the case? He'd always thought of his father as the head of the house, but that might've been because

Mom had said it so many times, not because they actually lived it. He'd store that one away to think over later. "Come on, Dad. The twins must've gotten their love of adventure from somewhere." And it hadn't been Lisa. "I know I can hardly wait to go."

"I…"

"Plus, isn't this thing very expensive?" asked Mom. "How many people are you paying for?"

Cameron shrugged. "We're not taking a bunch of their young friends, if that's what you're worried about. Alaina said they'd have a little party at the summer program on their birthday, same as they do for any child. No gifts, but they do get cupcakes and candles, and everyone sings 'Happy Birthday.' It's not like the boys need more ten-dollar junk to wreck and throw away, anyway. I'd rather give them an experience they'll remember for their entire lives." Maybe he should explain a bit more. "I make good money, Mom. I'm happy to pay for you and Dad. I'm paying for Alaina, the boys, and myself as it is. If you don't think you can afford it and want to come anyway, please let me help out." Although he'd helped out plenty by giving them a rent-free place to live over the summer. Not that it had cost him anything, other than the power bill.

Mom's lips tightened. "When are you going to give up on taunting us with this young woman?"

Cameron kept his gaze and voice steady. "I'm not taunting. I love Alaina, and she loves me. I'm only telling you how things are."

"So you're not at all bothered by the fact that you're about to commit adultery? If you haven't already, that is."

Cameron counted to ten inside his head — then fifty — before he trusted his voice. "I have not committed adultery, Mom, and I have no intention of doing so. I plan to marry Alaina, if she'll have me, and when we make love, it will be in the sanctity of marriage."

Dad tapped his pencil against the paper.

Some days Cameron felt like shoving that worthless wad of newsprint into the trash and seeing if he could ever get his dad to just talk to him, man to man. No wonder he counted so much on the men's group at church.

"Well, I guess we can't stop you." Mom bit off each word.

"No, you can't." Even acknowledging it out loud untethered a little bit of freedom to float in Cameron's soul. "Although the honest truth is that I would like your blessing. I would like you to be happy for me and the boys, that we've found someone to share our life with."

His mother's glare said it all.

Well, at least Cameron had gotten it off his chest. He hadn't really hoped for anything more — not out of the blue like that — but a man could always hope. When push came to shove, hope was all any of them had.

"So, about Zip the Snake. We're going next Sunday after lunch. It's down in the canyon near the golf course in Twin Falls, and there's a park nearby along the Snake River. I thought we might have a picnic after everyone who wants to has ridden the zip line. So if the two of you don't want to ride, you're welcome to meet us at Centennial Park at 4:30. I'll even leave the picnic coolers with you in that case, instead of leaving them in the car for the duration of the ride. The weather is supposed to be quite hot."

"On Sunday?" Mom's face drew into an even deeper scowl.

"Yes. We're not skipping church, so don't worry about that. They have a big tour group coming through on Saturday, so they didn't have any openings for a group the size of ours. Sunday afternoon works just as well for us."

His parents exchanged a look, and Dad's head gave a quick shake.

"We'll meet you at the park, then, I guess." Mom pursed her lips. "There is no way I am strapping into some flimsy harness and flinging myself across the river. I don't know in what universe anyone could think that would be a fun thing to do."

Cameron chuckled. "Two things. One, the ride doesn't actually go *across* the Snake. It's in the canyon beside it... but your point is well taken. And, second, you sound so much like Grady did a year and half ago. Poor guy had such a fear of heights, you wouldn't believe it."

"It's not heights I'm afraid of..." Mom's voice petered out. "Okay, maybe it is. But it's way too much money to spend on anyone who doesn't really want to do it, don't you think?"

Cameron shrugged. "I'm willing to foot the bill, and you two can chalk it up to life experience. Come on. Live a little dangerously. Just think of the stories you can tell your Bible school students when you get back to England. You'll gain their respect in a whole new way."

Dad rose to his feet. "We already have their respect. And I'm not sure what kind of spiritual lesson you can think of to learn from riding a zip line. I'm having none of it. Nora, let's go downstairs."

"Fine." Mom looked between her husband and her son and headed down the basement stairs.

Their footsteps faded as they descended. Cameron stared at the closed door. That had actually gone somewhat better than he expected. Not that he'd ever thought they would jump at the chance to ride Zip the Snake, but he thought they might spend more time insisting on an age-appropriate party for the boys. What he hadn't told his parents yet was that they'd invited several of their friends' families to come. Alaina was even going to ask her parents. Cameron grinned. That was something he'd pay good money to see.

Chapter 20

"WHEEE!" EVAN SQUEALED with delight as the zip line deposited him to the bottom of the fourth run.

Alaina couldn't help the laughter bubbling out of her as she helped the little boy out of his harness. "You liked that, did you?"

Evan threw his arms around her and gave her a big hug. "That was so much fun! Can we do it again? Please?"

"That's it for today, buddy. Everybody gets to ride all four zip lines one time, and then that's the end of the fun for this visit."

"But when can we do it again?"

Alaina felt Cameron's presence even before his hand rested on her shoulder. "We'll find another time. Don't worry. But we won't do it every week."

Alaina rose from her crouch, thrilled to feel Cameron's hand still on her. His other hand reached for his son and tousled his hair. Then he looked around at the gathering. This fourth zip line allowed two riders to slide side-by-side. Alaina's parents were on the downhill approach, the last of their group.

Alaina met her mother's eyes as she began to unbuckle. "What did you think, Mom?"

Mom rested a hand across her heart and gave a wobbly smile. "Well, I can cross that off my bucket list."

Alaina chuckled and glanced at her dad. "Pretty fun, huh?"

Dad stepped away out of his harness and slid his arm around Mom. "I've always wondered what that would be like, and now I know." He gave Mom's shoulder a squeeze. "You don't want to do it again, Louise?"

"Not very badly," Mom admitted. "But I'm glad I did it once."

Cameron turned Alaina so they were facing the rest of the group. "Everyone ready? Let's head over to Centennial Waterfront Park for our picnic. My parents should have everything set up. I'll just send them a quick text to let them know we'll be there in ten minutes or so."

Evan bounded off with Oliver and Maisie up the trail toward the parking lot. Everyone else followed more slowly. Grady and Joanna shared a long kiss as they strolled arm-in-arm, and Alaina grinned at the sight. Cameron had mentioned that Grady, who was terrified of heights, had proposed to Joanna right here on this zip line one day last summer. Good for him for repeating the ride. It looked like it brought back great memories for both of them.

Cameron drew her close. "So, what did you think? Something you'd like to do again?"

She slipped her arm around his waist as they fell into step behind everyone else. "It was a lot of fun. I've always loved roller coasters and the like, so it shouldn't be all that surprising for me. How about you?" She tilted her head toward him. "Have you done this before?"

He kept his eyes fixed on hers. "Yep."

So, something else he'd shared with Lisa. Well, she'd gone whitewater rafting with Garth. It wasn't like she could erase the memories they'd shared, even if she wanted to. She was pretty sure Cameron and his ex-wife must've had some great times together, or they wouldn't have stayed married for five years. Just like she and Garth had had some great times, too. But she was oh-so-ready to move on and put Garth in the rearview mirror. Truthfully, he'd been there for months already.

Cameron dipped his head toward her and gave her a quick kiss. "But this was more fun. I loved sharing today with you and the twins. Ollie was a tiny bit nervous, but once we got going, he loved it as much as Evan did."

Alaina couldn't help but tease. "But did we have to share it with so many *other* people?" She hoped her twinkling eyes would alert him that she hadn't minded. She really hadn't, but the thought of zipping sometime with just her and Cameron sounded pretty fun, too.

Cameron grinned at her. "If it hadn't been for the boys' birthday, it would've been different. We'll have more chances... although, truth be told, the boys would be supremely unimpressed if we zipped very often without them."

One more reminder that Cameron and his sons were a package deal. A few weeks ago, that had bothered her far more than it did now. She'd seen how adept Cameron was at figuring out ways for just the two of them to spend time together while not neglecting his sons. Surely he would keep that in mind as time went on.

Her heart stilled at the thought. Everything in their relationship hinted toward the fact that he was going to ask her to marry him, only how long would he make her wait? How sure was he that this was the right thing to do? Was he going to wait until his parents came around? Because she could die a lonely death of old age while waiting for them to have a change of heart.

She tipped her head toward his and pulled him to a stop. She wrapped both arms around his waist. "I love you, Cameron Kraus. You are an awesome dad and a pretty good boyfriend, besides."

"Pretty good, huh?" He kissed her nose lightly. "I was hoping for something a little more solid than that. Best in the world, perhaps. Or maybe something like, 'there's no one else in the universe for me'." His eyes gleamed as he looked deep into her soul.

Alaina's heart caught in her throat. "Now that you mention it, that's exactly what I meant. There's no one else I want beside me. Ever."

She barely got the last word out before his mouth covered hers. Her heart rate kicked up a notch as his lips caressed hers with all the confidence in the world. No one else — not even Garth — had ever made her feel like this. So loved. So desired. So beautiful. She could stand in his arms all day, giving this sweet kiss back the same way he was offering it to her.

They belonged together. No question.

"Hey, are you guys coming?" Joanna's voice, calling

from above, was filled with laughter.

Cameron turned Alaina so that his body shielded the view of them from the rest of the group. She could feel his lips tilting up at the corners as he gave her one last kiss. "We'll finish this later," he murmured.

She liked the sound of that.

Cameron drove into the lot at Centennial Waterfront Park and parked beside his parents' car. The rest of the group was just arriving as his parents waved from the nearby picnic table.

In the backseat, he could already hear the unclicking of belt buckles as the twins freed themselves then hurried out of the car.

"Shut the doors!" he called.

Both boys dashed back and slammed the car doors before Cameron could so much extract himself from the vehicle himself. He rounded the car and opened the door for Alaina. "Ready?" he whispered.

She looked past his arm, visibly swallowed, then glanced up at him with a small smile. "As ready as I'm going to get."

They'd prayed together earlier, not for the first time, that things would improve with his parents. Was it too much to hope for an about-face right now, today? He let out a long breath as he and Alaina walked toward the picnic shelter, hand-in-hand. Dad glanced over at them then away, nothing registering on his facial expression. How could his father keep that mask on all the time? For once, Mom didn't have anything to say. She pursed her lips and glared at him, but that was the end of it. She probably didn't want to make a scene in front of everyone else, though it had rarely stopped her before.

Cameron managed another breath. The miracle he had been praying for hadn't happened yet, but there was still plenty of time for God to get everything worked out. Within his heart, he had no doubts. God had the situation under control and was testing their faith.

"This looks like quite a feast, son." Alaina's dad, Duane, clapped his hand on Cameron's shoulder. Cameron reeled, both from the firm clout and from the use of the word 'son.' Sounded like Duane was sending a not-so-subtle message to Cameron's own father.

"I hope there's lots. Let's see, we've got all the taco fixings here from El Corazon. Mom picked up the birthday cake from Demi's Delights. And then, of course, we have lots of chips from Stargil, and some of that great eggplant dip from the farmers market." He shot a grin at Ben. "Had that at your house the first time, man. Good stuff."

"We sure like it." Ben grinned.

Maisie made a gagging motion, and Ben squeezed his stepdaughter to his side. "Hey, come on, sweetie. I thought you liked it."

"Not very much." She looked over at Cameron. "Is there salsa, too?"

Cameron chuckled. "Sure is." He looked around the group and squeezed Alaina's hand. "Dad, would you ask the blessing, please? I know it would mean a lot to Ollie and Evan."

His dad's startled gaze met his. "Okay." He cleared his throat. "If everyone could please bow their heads and close their eyes. Dear heavenly Father, we thank Thee for this beautiful day and for the twins' birthday. We ask that Thou wilt bless this food to our bodies and bless these young men in their new year. Amen."

His parents had already spread the food out along the picnic table with paper plates and plastic cutlery at one end. Several gallons of iced tea stood at the other end, surrounded by stacks of plastic cups. Cameron felt a stab of guilt. Probably, if Alaina had been in charge, they wouldn't be using disposables. But, hey, he was a bachelor, and there was a limit to what he could manage on any given day. Today, he was just hoping everyone would come through unscathed. At least no one had been injured on the zip line. That was a good start.

Two more cars pulled into the parking lot, and a whole bunch of old ladies poured out.

Cameron recognized Enid Bigby and some of her friends, and waved with a small smile. This group must be the infamous Grannies, known across Arcadia Valley as an intrepid group of octogenarians who lived with the motto 'no fear' or something like that. He'd heard tales of their escapades, some of which even made the Valley Times.

Several of the women waved and a few people in both parties exchanged greetings. They opened cartons heaped with fried chicken at their table, each old woman talking faster and louder than all the others until their voices and laughter made it nearly impossible for his own group to hear each other.

Dad twisted in his lawn chair to glare at them over his shoulder. He opened his mouth to say something, but then his face paled and he whipped right back around, his hands shaking slightly as he reached for his tumbler of iced tea.

Interesting. Wonder what that was all about? Cameron let his gaze land on each granny at a time until he came to Mona Henderson. Her narrowed eyes seemed to be focused on the back of Dad's head. Then she slowly rose and stalked toward their table. She had all the grace one might expect of an old lady who rode a motorcycle and went bungee jumping.

"Wilfred Kraus, is that you?" Dad's face paled and his eyes closed for so long Cameron wondered if his dad had fainted dead away, but that couldn't be right. His dad had only visited Arcadia Valley briefly a few times before. How could Mona possibly know him?

Chapter 21

ALAINA GLANCED UP at Cameron, but he seemed to be just as surprised as she was. Talk at both tables dwindled. Okay, it dwindled at their table, but at the other one, it ended abruptly with Enid Bigby's curt word, "Silence!"

Everyone's eyes seemed trained on Nora and Wilfred Kraus. As though in slow motion, Cameron's dad gathered himself and rose to his feet, steadying himself against the picnic table before he opened his eyes. "Hello? Have we met?"

Alaina looked at Cameron as he shook his head. It seemed obvious his dad's bluff was useless.

"Oh, I'm pretty sure we have, Sonny. Seems to me you've aged a bit since the last time, so your memory might be shot." She cackled. "It was down in Redding, California, when you were drooling around my daughter Brenda like a puppy over a juicy bone." She leaned closer, peering up at him from a height of little over five feet.

Nora Kraus gasped then her hand quickly rose to cover her mouth.

"Redding?" Wilfred asked, his voice faint.

Was the man going to have a heart attack on the spot? Alaina wasn't completely sure — she looked around the group, trying to remember who had the most first-aid experience. That might be her, what with lifeguarding years ago and within the early childhood system since. Her training had mostly been about drowning and choking hazards for children, though. Not so much middle-aged men having heart failure.

"I told her no good could possibly come from sleeping with you," Mona went on. "You're just lucky she never got pregnant or contracted one of those sexy diseases, is all I can say. I've kept an eye on your career from time to time and wondered how you could live with yourself." Hands on her hips, Mona looked around their table, her gaze finally setting on Cameron's. She jerked her chin toward him. "I don't hold it against you what your father did. You seem like a decent young man. Those boys of yours rode that zip line real well. They're not chicken like their grandfather." She tucked her fists in her armpits and flapped her arms. With a final "Bok Bok" she stalked back to her table.

The Grannies' chatter resumed, thankfully not as quite as loudly as before. At the twins' birthday celebration, however, no one spoke a word as Cameron's dad lowered himself back into his lawn chair, face ashen and eyes clenched shut.

Alaina all but held her breath. Surely everyone wondered the same thing she did. Exactly when was it that Wilfred Kraus had had an affair? Because there seemed to be no doubt Mona Henderson had spoken the truth, or he would have refuted her.

Cameron's fingers disentangled themselves from hers then his arm wrapped around her waist. She leaned against him for what comfort they could share.

"Wilfred?" Nora Kraus's voice was strident. "In Redding?"

"I can explain," murmured Wilfred.

"Well, I, for one, would like to hear it."

"Later."

Nora leaned into Wilfred's face, grasped him by both shoulders, and gave him a shake. "Oh, no, you don't. I'm not thrilled she said it in public, but she did. I've always wondered what happened in Redding, and now I know. And so does everyone else, so there's no use in having this discussion privately later."

Wilfred's hands covered his wife's hands on his shoulders. "I didn't mean to, honey. I really didn't, but you and the children were so far away, and I was lonely."

Alaina felt Cameron's sharp intake of breath as much as she heard it. This was worse than she'd thought at first. She'd wondered if it had been before his marriage to Nora, perhaps even before he met her. But this was much, much worse. Not only had he been married, but they already had a family.

"How does being lonely make a difference, Dad?" Cameron's voice shook as he toggled his finger between his parents. "You've been telling me that my chance at happiness within the bounds of marriage — or anywhere — are over because Lisa divorced me. You have the nerve to say that when you had an affair when you were married?" He leaned closer, but Alaina did not relinquish her grip around his middle.

"I never cheated on Lisa. Not even once. Was I ever tempted to?" He gave a short laugh. "Sure, just to spite her, not because I fancied myself in love with anyone else. Not simply because I was *lonely*."

Wilfred's eyes met Cameron's, a depth of sorrow welling in them. "I'm sorry, son. So sorry."

Nora turned on her heel and strode away across the parking lot. She climbed into their car and skidded out in a peel of gravel. No one spoke for a long moment at their table.

"Dad, can I have another taco?"

Cameron let out a long breath as he focused on his son. "Sure, Ollie. Let's get you one."

Later that evening, after Cameron had dropped off Alaina and put the boys in bed, he waited for his sister. He'd been holding his anger, his frustration, and his twenty million questions under check for the past several hours, and it was time to get some answers. Joanna's car pulled up at the curb, and they went downstairs together. Cameron gave a sharp knock on the basement door.

The door opened, and Mom's haggard face greeted them. She looked from Cameron to Joanna and back again, her shoulders slumping. "I should have known you'd come."

Joanna stepped forward and wrapped her arms around their mother. "Of course, we came. We're not here to satisfy our curiosity, but because we're a family, and families stick together. We want you to know we're here for you and will support you both."

Joanna could sound like she didn't care about the details, but Cameron certainly did. He could hardly believe it, after all these years. After all that sermonizing. Yes, he'd prayed that God would crack the situation wide open. But he'd certainly never expected it to happen this way.

Joanna released their mother and stepped around her to their father, who stood at the other end of the kitchen. He looked like he'd aged twenty years in the past few hours.

Mom looked up at Cameron. He took a deep breath, slung his arm over her shoulders, and gave a little hug. "Hey, Mom."

She hugged him back and pulled him toward the small sitting room where the other two had already disappeared. Dad sank into the recliner, while Mom and Joanna settled into the loveseat. Cameron took the one remaining chair and lowered himself into it. He leaned forward, elbows on his knees, hands clasped in front of him, as he looked from one parent to the other. "Go ahead, Dad."

Joanna glanced over at him. "Cameron, would you mind saying a prayer before we get started?"

Did he mind? Oh, he minded all right. But she was right. He'd learned to rely so much on his heavenly Father over the past few years that he didn't want his shock and anger at his earthly one to take any of that peace away.

He gave a curt nod and prayed out loud, asking for God's truth and healing and guidance to be clear. When he was done, he raised his eyebrows and looked back at his father.

"There's not much to tell." Dad's eyes darted between the three of them, lingering longest on Mom. "I was away from home for two months. It was during the time we lived

196

in San Antonio." He winced. "I'd gone to Redding to get some of the training under my belt for teaching Bible school."

Yeah, that admission should be wince-worthy. "So, how did she seduce you?" Cameron had trouble keeping the bitterness out of his voice but, God knew, he tried.

"She was a waitress at the diner a bunch of us went to often. She was a bit flirty, but it was only in fun, at least at first." Dad's hand passed over his eyes as he paused. "One night, when I was feeling particularly vulnerable, I stayed at the café until closing. I walked out with her as she locked up and, well, one thing led to another."

Mom's fingers picked at the afghan on the loveseat with such determination that Cameron was afraid she'd unravel the entire thing. But, man, if this was such a shock to him and Joanna, what must it be like for his mother? Maybe he should be feeling a bit more sympathy for her.

Joanna leaned forward. "So it was a one-time thing?"

Dad shook his head, not meeting anyone's gaze.

Cameron surged to his feet. "Seriously? You were a married man with a family, a Christian man, pursuing divinity studies. And you knowingly and consciously slept with another woman? More than once? I don't get it, Dad. I really don't."

"Let him finish, Cameron," said Joanna softly.

He whirled around. "What else is there to say? It doesn't matter to me if he was drunk, overwhelmed by her beauty and wit, or anything in between. He betrayed Mom. He betrayed you and me. And yet, all these years, he's pontificated about being a righteous man with a good reputation. What can he possibly say to refute all that?" Cameron took a deep breath, let it out, and shook his head. He headed for the door.

"Son, wait."

His mom's voice. Cameron paused, halfway across the kitchen, and sent a silent prayer heavenward. *God? Why should I listen to more?*

And yet, obedience to his parents was entrenched. *Help me, Lord. I'm as likely to fly off the handle as not. I don't think I can trust my voice. All I know is I don't want to say anything that I'll have to apologize for later. Guard my mouth, Lord, please.*

He turned back and resumed his seat in the easy chair, gritting his teeth.

Joanna gave him a small smile and took their mother's hand between both of hers. "Now I want to hear from you. Were you being faithful? Looking back, was there any sign that this was about to happen or had happened?"

Cameron closed his eyes. If there was more wrong with his parents' marriage, then or now, he didn't even want to know about it. But the silence went on so long that he had to look. His parents were having one of those silent conversations with their eyes that no offspring could ever hope to read.

Mom's shoulders shook. "No, I didn't have an affair myself, but someone spread a rumor after I had coffee with our church's minister of music a few times. It started out with me discussing upcoming solos with him, but I'll admit I appreciated the fact that he would talk to me as though I were a real person. Your father was always so busy, so focused on his work. But I promise you, nothing ever happened. After the gossip went out, I knew I was at the point where I had to make a decision. I chose not to meet that man alone anymore. I chose your father, our family."

So many things Cameron had never wanted to know about his parents. He tried to think of them as young and attractive and filled with the desire for companionship, for love. His imagination failed him.

Joanna squeezed their mother's hands. "So, what happens next? If you never guessed that Dad had an affair all those years ago, can you forgive him now?"

Dad stumbled to his feet then knelt beside Mom at the loveseat, grappling for her hands. "Please, Nora. I'm so sorry. I should've told you. It should never have happened. I've regretted it every single day in all these years. Can you ever forgive me?"

The fate of the universe hung in the balance. Cameron held his breath.

Mom's hands folded tightly in her lap as she stared into his eyes. "I need a bit of time, Wilfred. I don't know how to take this in."

Chapter 22

SHE'D WAITED AND WAITED for Cameron's text last night, pacing the floor of the cottage until well past midnight before crawling into bed. Finally she'd fallen asleep…and somehow missed the chime of his incoming text at 1:34.

What a mess. That could've gone better. I'll fill you in tomorrow.

That was it?

Now Alaina stared, unseeing, at her computer. With the summer program two-thirds completed, the next round of programming required her attention. They'd be switching to preschool and after-school activities the third week of August in one section of the renovated house, with the daycare operating in the remaining space. Registrations were queued up to be finalized, and several résumés were on file for the additional staff member they needed to hire.

She needed to focus. But what was going on with Cameron's parents? His mom had left the picnic in an understandable huff, leaving a withdrawn Wilfred to get a ride back to Arcadia Valley with Joanna and Grady. The silence hadn't been remarkable in itself. That pair didn't usually feel the need to say anything unless they were cutting someone else's dreams off at the knees.

Okay, so she shouldn't be bitter about them. Obviously they had really big issues to deal with.

Alaina glanced at the clock. Never had a day gone slower that she could remember but, finally, it was nearly over. She rubbed her eyes and squinted at her monitor. And yet, even then, she couldn't focus. Cameron often worked late on Mondays, leaving Nora to pick up the boys. Would she be here today? What kind of 'not really well' had last night been like, anyway? She could only imagine.

She'd have some really big issues herself if she didn't get her work done. Outside the window, open to the late July breeze, she could hear children's voices as they called to one another in the playground.

A car pulled into the parking lot, its tires crunching on the gravel. Pick-up time already? Alaina reached for her clipboard and walked into the other room.

Dina Poncetta's gloating face met hers.

Great. She must have heard about Cameron's parents. Probably the whole town had by now. Centennial Waterfront Park wasn't exactly a private venue, nor were the Grannies noted for keeping secrets.

"Oh, how the high and mighty have fallen."

"Good afternoon, Dina. Here to pick up the girls?" Alaina kept her voice pleasant. Professional.

"Just wait until I tell Lisa what happened. She'll think it's pretty funny. They never liked her, you know."

Alaina's smile froze. "Oh, you and Lisa are friends?"

"Yes, we go way back. My husband works over at Stargil, head of the production line, where Cameron is an accountant. And you know what they say about accountants." She rolled her eyes.

Why were they having this conversation? Alaina backed up a step and held out the clipboard.

"Narrow-minded. Rigid. Lisa couldn't live that way anymore, with a stick-in-the-mud who thought the definition of fun was binge-solving Sudoku."

Cameron was a lot of fun. Romantic dinners at one end of the spectrum and zip lining on the other. So he liked number puzzles. It could be useful having an accountant around at tax time.

Alaina raised her eyebrows. "Your point is?"

"You seem like a decent person, Alaina. I just feel you should be warned. He once swept Lisa off her feet, too, but it turned out all he really wanted was someone to run his household so he could work overtime. Lisa stuck it out for a while because of the money, but he drove her bat-crazy, thinking she should stay home and keep the house clean, even though he could totally afford to hire someone."

Didn't most people clean their own homes? But, yeah, her parents shared those duties. Dad did more than mow the lawn and take out the garbage.

Dina leaned closer. "I just thought you should be aware that his whole family tries so hard to look good on the outside, but they're not that great behind the mask. Even Joanna. Her old boyfriend in Salt Lake City said she'd tried to blackmail him."

Joanna? Grady's wife? Dina had to be wrong about that, and Alaina shouldn't even be listening to all this poison. She tapped the clipboard and pivoted for the patio doors. "The girls are in the playground."

"I can't marry you if you can't cook."

Alaina jerked to a stop and stared at Evan. He stood a few inches from Ophelia, staring in her face. "Cooking's a girl job," he went on.

"Evan Kraus!" Alaina's voice sounded squeaky, even to herself. "That's not how we talk around here."

From behind her, Dina snickered. "Just like his dad. Don't say I didn't warn you." She stepped around Alaina. "Seven-year-olds don't need to worry about getting married, so enough of that, okay? Come along, Ophelia."

Evan shrugged before climbing the monkey bars as the little girl ran toward her mother. Dina initialed the check-out sheet and gave Alaina a smug smile. "I didn't set that up," she murmured as she swept past.

Alaina pressed her hand against her chest as she watched Dina and her daughters leave the daycare. She should think of something to say to Evan, but what? It wasn't her place — not yet, anyway — to correct his misconceptions.

Her office phone was ringing when she went back inside. "Grace Greenhouse, Miss Alaina speaking."

"Alaina, I'm glad you picked up. It's Cameron. I hate to ask this of you, but something's come up at work, and I won't be able to get away for a few hours. Mom and Joanna are out of town, and Dad's a mess. Any chance I can get you to take the boys home? I'll fill you in on everything when I get home later."

... but it turned out all he really wanted was someone to run his household so he could work overtime. Dina's words ricocheted through her mind. No, that's not how it was. Alaina knew him better than that. If he had an emergency at work, he had an emergency at work.

"I can do that."

But her heart wasn't so sure.

⌖

Man, all he'd wanted had been to pick up Alaina and the boys from Grace, grab a bag of takeout, and spend the evening together. He needed to let her know what all had gone down with his parents the night before.

Now the evening glow had settled over Arcadia Valley, and she'd texted to say she'd tucked the boys in bed. There'd been no time for him to explain anything at all. Not to let her know why his family was unavailable to the boys.

The flower garden across the front of his house looked well-kept — thanks to Mom — as he pulled up. A sweet fragrance filled the air, and he stopped to inhale deeply with his eyes closed. *Thank you, Jesus, that this day is over, and yesterday with it.*

The front door opened, and Alaina stood silhouetted against the living room light. "Cameron, is that you?"

What would it be like to come home to her every day? For her to have supper cooked and on the table, for the boys to be home and happy, for the house to be tidy, and all the other good stuff that came with having a loving, attentive wife? Lisa hadn't been as much into all of those things as he'd hoped, but the love he shared with Alaina seemed deeper already after only two short months.

He climbed the steps and wrapped his arms around her, drinking in the sweet magnolia scent of her, and feeling her soft curls swish against his arms. He bent and kissed her, savoring the moment. "Any leftovers for me?"

Alaina leaned back, smiling at him. "Didn't you order something into the office? The boys and I picked up hotdogs from the Jukebox on our way over."

Now that was a date he wished he could've gone on. "No worries. I'll find something in the fridge, I'm sure." It wouldn't be as good as a loaded hotdog and French fries shared with those he loved best.

"What happened with your parents later on?" Alaina followed him into the kitchen.

"Just a sec." Cameron opened the fridge and found the leftover burritos he'd planned to take for his lunch tomorrow. Oh, well, he'd stop at the drive-through in the morning and get something else. He set the container in the microwave and tapped a button. "Thanks for filling in for my boys. Are they asleep?"

She nodded. "Yes, they've been in bed for over an hour. I was wondering how much longer you would be."

The microwave beeped, and Cameron reached inside for his plate. He set it on the table and beckoned her to join him. He took a few bites then got up and raided the fridge for salsa. "Let me tell you what happened last night. That was crazy."

Alaina nodded, her dark brown eyes fixed on his. "I was pretty shocked by what Mona said, and even more shocked when it seemed to be true."

She could say that again. After all those years growing up listening to his parents talk about keeping himself pure and being a man of honor, he had a hard time adjusting to reality himself.

"My mother is having a really hard time forgiving Dad, and I can't say that I blame her. She said she needed to go away for a few days but, in the state of mind she was in, I didn't think it was a very good idea." Cameron smeared salsa on his food. "Neither did Joanna, so she took Mom to her house last night. They drove to Salt Lake City this morning. Joanna booked a Bed and Breakfast for them for a few days."

Alaina regarded him thoughtfully. "That's really a good thing your sister did."

"Mom isn't all that easy to live with." Cameron forced a chuckle. "Well, I guess you figured that part out. But she is our mother, and she needs us right now."

"How about your dad?" Alaina asked softly.

"He's in the basement, as far as I know. I talked to him once today, and figured I'd stop down there yet this evening." Cameron shook his head and let out a long sigh. "Right now I feel like they're my children as surely as Ollie and Evan. And parenting them is three times as hard."

"I'm so sorry."

He managed a small grin. "About the only good thing I can see coming from all this is that it will be increasingly difficult for the pot to call the kettle black."

She shook her head, smiling slightly. "That has crossed my mind, but it didn't seem like a gracious thought to have."

"I hear you. It's not the way I wished things would go down. I mean, something needed to give way, but I sure wasn't expecting something like this."

Alaina straightened a stack of Sudoku puzzle books on the corner of the table. "Your parents have always been rather traditional, haven't they?"

She needed to ask? Wasn't the evidence in every word they'd spoken? "You could say that."

"So, your dad teaches Bible school." She glanced up at him. "What does your mom do?"

"She keeps their place clean, invites students over for meals, leads a women's Bible study. That kind of thing."

Alaina's smile was more like a grimace. "Practically the perfect wife."

Cameron leaned back in his chair and chuckled. "I don't think I'd put it that way. Can you imagine living with either one of them? They put on a good front for the ministry, but they had quite a mess behind closed doors."

"Yeah."

"Thanks for picking up the slack tonight, sweetheart." He waved his fork around the kitchen then scraped up the last bite of burrito. "You can see how much the boys and I need a woman's touch around here. We need someone to take care of us. We love you, Alaina, and we need you."

One day soon he'd tell her more than that. Once all this mess was past them. There was going to be a sunrise, and soon.

Cameron set his plate in the sink and turned to Alaina, but she stayed seated, searching his gaze. For what? He didn't know.

He stopped behind her, gathering her curly locks out of the way before massaging her shoulders gently. "Sweetheart?

What are you thinking?"

Alaina pulled to her feet and out of his grasp. "I need to go. It's been a really long couple of days."

He stood in the middle of the kitchen for a long moment after the sound of her car drifted away. What had happened there, anyway?

Chapter 23

NOT FOR THE FIRST TIME, Alaina paced the small living room the cottage she shared with Kenia. "If I didn't know better, I could swear he's looking for a housekeeper more than a wife."

Kenia sat curled up in her armchair, a bowl of popcorn in her lap. "Why would you say that? I thought you told me how much you love him and how much he loves you."

"I'm having second thoughts, okay?" Alaina pivoted in front of the fridge and turned to face her roommate. "He asked me what was for dinner, if you can believe it. It's not like I told him I was going to cook a meal. He said he had to work late and his parents and sister couldn't step in for the boys. Okay. But, apparently I was supposed to read his mind and cook a three-course dinner for him? He didn't even let me know how late he'd be." She gave a sharp laugh. "I don't know what to make of it."

"It's not like the last few days have been normal for him

and his family." Kenia picked up a kernel of popcorn, tossed it in the air, and caught it in her mouth.

"No, you're right. He's under a lot of stress right now. But how does that saying go? It's when you're in hot water that your true colors come out."

"I think you might be reading too much into this."

"Am I, really? His mom does all that and more for his father. She's the perfect little housekeeper wife. She can cook, bake, and can tomatoes with the best of them. Probably with one hand tied behind her back."

"So, now you're jealous of Nora Kraus? Now you want to be just like her when you grow up?"

Alaina snorted. "As if. But I can't shake the feeling that she's exactly what Cameron is looking for. Dina Poncetta told me how he treated Lisa, as though he wanted his mother to live in or something."

"Just like many of us, Cameron has a before and an after. Remember how much he's changed since his marriage with Lisa. Not that you knew him then, of course, but I did."

It was hard to argue against Kenia. She was right. "I don't know. I just realized today there are big warning signs flashing all around me, and I've been ignoring them. My parents were more concerned about me becoming a stepmother. And, after spending all evening with the twins without Cameron around, I can tell you there would be some challenges with that."

"Would be?" Kenia asked softly.

Alaina squeezed her eyes shut, trying to keep hot tears from leaking out. "Yeah. I just don't know if I can do this."

"May I give you a suggestion?"

"Like I can stop you."

Kenia chuckled. "I'll forget you said that. You're the one who came in needing to talk, remember?"

"I'm sorry. You're right. Carry on."

"Remember that you don't have to make any life-changing decisions today, okay? You have time to pray about it, time to see how things work out with Cameron's parents, time to analyze if that's really the kind of man he will turn out to be. There's no hurry."

"Okay. You're right." She turned and headed for her bedroom, but before she could turn the knob, Kenia's voice came again.

"I'll be praying for you, sweet friend."

Wasn't it just a week or two ago Alaina had thought Kenia was the wild one? How did her friend suddenly seem to make so much sense?

It was Wednesday after supper before Joanna and Mom pulled back up to the curb in front of Cameron's house. He glanced over at his dad. "They're home."

Dad hadn't had a whole lot to say since they'd left. He'd spent the past two evenings upstairs, working puzzles and reading the paper until he nearly drove Cameron crazy. It seemed they'd both been waiting for the other shoe to drop.

Through the window, Joanna popped the trunk and retrieved Mom's carry-on. Both of them started down the walk toward the basement entrance, but Cameron opened his door. "Dad's in here. The boys are outside on the trampoline."

Joanna and Mom exchanged a look and turned up the main sidewalk. Cameron stepped aside to allow them entrance. In his periphery, he saw Dad stumble to his feet.

Cameron whispered a prayer. He wasn't sure how much more drama he could manage. He'd talk to Alaina on the phone a couple of times, but she'd been quiet and hadn't seemed eager to come over, and he hadn't felt like he had any other option but to stay near Dad. Not with everything that was going on.

Dad shuffled up beside Cameron. "Hi, Nora. Did you girls have a good getaway?"

Mom stopped in the doorway, but Joanna nudged her forward until she could get the door closed behind them both. "Hello, Wilfred. We had a fine time, thank you."

Cameron looked at her sister with eyebrows raised. No clues yet as to how this was going to play out.

Joanna shook her head slightly and set down the carry-on. "Well, I should be going now. Grady is waiting for me."

"No, please." Mom grabbed for Joanna's hand. "Just a bit longer, please."

At his sister's nod, Cameron felt like he could breathe again. He wanted to know what was going on, but he didn't want to be the only witness.

Dad stretched both hands in front of him. "Nora? Will you forgive me?"

Well, at least he wasn't beating around the bush. The answer would be out sooner rather than later.

"Wilfred, I won't lie. These past few days have been the

most difficult in my life. I feel like everything we've ever lived for, every advice we've ever given, every Bible study we've ever led has been a pretense. A sham."

Dad hung his head. If possible, his face was even grayer than it had been before. "I know," he whispered. "I can't tell you how very sorry I am."

"What I want to know is — are you truly sorry it happened, or are you only sorry you got caught? How could you live with yourself all these years? How could you do this to me?" Mom's voice rose a bit with each question.

Dad reached for the back of the loveseat to hold him up. "I didn't know how to tell you all those years ago, and then, when I confessed my sin to God, so much time had passed that it didn't seem relevant anymore."

"Oh, it was relevant, Wilfred."

"I'm sorry, Nora. You're the only woman I've ever loved."

"But not the only woman you've ever slept with," Mom said bitterly.

Dad looked down at the floor. "I can see now I should have found a way to tell you a long time ago."

Mom took a couple of steps closer and rested her hands on her hips. "You can see that now, can you? They say hindsight is twenty-twenty, but it still makes me wonder if I would've gone to the grave not knowing this had ever happened."

Pretty sure she guessed right, thought Cameron, watching his dad's face.

"So, if you hate me so much now, why did you come home today?"

Mom's lips thinned as she shook her head. "You want to know something, Wilfred? You're a fool. Once, many years ago, I promised to love you for richer and for poorer, in sickness and in health, as long as we both shall live. I figure that as much as I hate you right now, I still love you, and a vow is a vow."

Cameron turned away. Of course she'd throw those words out in front of him, as though they made a difference when Lisa walked away. Hadn't those vows also included words like 'loving you above all others?' In his deepest heart, he'd barely dared to hope that this huge trial in his parents' marriage would make them more sympathetic to his own plight.

Should've known better.

Alaina worked alongside a volunteer group from the community at the garden beds. There was so much produce ripening every single day that it was hard to keep up.

"Thanks so much for helping today." Evelyn paused beside her carrying a basket loaded with fresh peppers and eggplant.

"No problem. It's not like I had anywhere else to be."

Evelyn gave her a sharp look. "Trouble in paradise?"

"You could say that."

"Want to talk about it?"

Alaina shook her head. "Not really." She heaved a big sigh.

"Let me drop off these vegetables at the truck, and I'll come pick beside you."

That's what she got for not being upbeat and thrilled to be here. She should've told Kenia she didn't have time to volunteer. Not that her roommate would've believed her.

A few minutes later Evelyn knelt on the path beside her and leaned into the garden bed. "Is it about Cameron's parents?"

"Kind of. But it's more than that." Man, she hadn't intended even to say that much.

"More than that, huh?"

"Just spending that time with his parents and seeing their trauma, and then—"

Evelyn cast her a sidelong glance. "Then what?"

Alaina sighed. "There's just been a lot going on. And through it all, I've come to wonder if I'm really the kind of person Cameron wants me to be."

"What kind of woman is that?"

Alaina shrugged. "You know. I get the feeling he'd like someone traditional, like his mother."

"I can't imagine anyone wanting to marry someone like Nora. No offense meant."

"I think what he really wants is the little woman. Someone to dust his house, do his laundry, fix his meals, that sort of thing."

Evelyn chuckled. "Don't we all?"

Alaina settled back on her heels and looked at her friend. "How come you didn't go out with Cameron last year?"

"Touché. He did seem a little more intense than I wanted to get involved with. He wanted to protect me and Maisie.

And, I don't know, we just weren't meant to be. We didn't love each other. You know?"

"Yeah, I know. My big question right now is whether *we* love each other enough. Or maybe, like him and you, we're just not meant to be."

"I can't answer that for you, but I will tell you that Cameron is a different person when he's around you. You've brought light, life, and laughter into his world, and I've seen the way he watches you. It's like you are the sun his world revolves around. He's not perfect, I'll grant you that. But neither is Ben. Neither am I, for that matter, or anyone else. We all make mistakes, and we all need forgiveness every single day. It's okay to take some time to think things over, for sure, but don't dismiss him at the first sign of trouble."

Alaina leaned over the garden bed and plucked out a small weed. "I feel like the summer has been so busy, and I haven't spent enough time praying about Cameron. I was so focused on proving his parents and mine wrong, and now it feels like the wind is out of my sails, and I don't know what to do next." She laughed, shaking her head. "That sounds terrible. But it's sort of true."

Evelyn pointed out a plant in the garden bed, loaded with red peppers. "Remember when these were little seedlings? We planted them in tiny peat pots in the greenhouse back in spring. When they each had just a small root, we transplanted them into bigger pots. Later, when their root systems were well-developed and the ground was warm enough, we transplanted them again into the garden."

"I remember." What was her friend getting at?

"I always think there's so many parallels between

gardening and being a believer. There are those verses in Ephesians chapter three, where Paul talks about being rooted and grounded in God's love. Have you read those lately?"

Alaina shook her head.

"They go like this in the New Living Translation." Evelyn grinned at her. "I memorized them because I needed to remember them constantly. 'Then Christ will make his home in your hearts as you trust in him. Your roots will grow down into God's love and keep you strong. And may you have the power to understand, as all God's people should, how wide, how long, how high, and how deep his love is. May you experience the love of Christ, though it is too great to understand fully. Then you will be made complete with all the fullness of life and power that comes from God.'"

"I'd forgotten about those verses," Alaina admitted.

"All I can say is to let your roots grow down into God's love. If you do that, you'll stay strong and understand everything you need to." Evelyn rose to her feet. "I'll be praying for you."

Was it so obvious to everyone that she needed it?

Chapter 24

*P*LEASE TELL ME you don't have plans for this evening." Cameron waited for Alaina to look up from her computer. "My mom is taking the boys home, and I'd like to take you out for dinner."

Just the sight of her sitting there, a vulnerable look on her face, crushed Cameron's heart. What had gone wrong? Why, after all this time, did he feel like she wouldn't welcome him if he strolled over and kissed her?

"I'm not sure." Alaina gathered her long curls in her hands and tossed them over her shoulder. She looked so pensive.

"Not sure about what? Not sure if you have plans?" He bit his lip. "Or is it that you're not sure you want to go out with me?" Because, every day this week, she'd come up with some reason not to spend time with him. Ever since the blowup at the boys' birthday party.

Alaina closed her eyes, her long lashes brushing her cheekbones, then looked at him again. "Maybe we could go out and talk."

"I guess that means Fire and Brimstone or The Jukebox are out." Cameron tried for a natural grin.

A small smile poked her dimple into her cheek. "Yeah. Too noisy."

He'd put off taking her to L'Aubergine for dinner, but maybe tonight was the night. He had a feeling their relationship was on the line, but he still couldn't figure out what he'd done wrong.

"Okay, I'll take the boys home now. Do you want me to pick you up from here at six or from the cottage a bit later?"

Alaina bit her lip. "Six-thirty at home?"

Cameron shoved his hands deeper into his shorts pockets. All he wanted to do was cross her office, gather her into his arms, and kiss her. He'd missed her so much, yet he'd seen her every day. But, if she was agreeable to dinner, that was a good start.

While he waited, he paced the living room. Mom poked around his kitchen, making dinner for her, Dad, and the twins. This time she had Dad cutting green beans into one-inch lengths. Huh. First time Cameron had ever seen his dad with a paring knife in his hands.

"Sit down, son. You're driving us all crazy with your pacing."

"Sorry, Mom. I'm nervous."

"It's rather obvious." Mom narrowed her gaze at Dad. "Is Alaina embarrassed to be seen with you after that public spectacle last Sunday?"

It *had* started about then. "I don't think that's it. I'm not sure what is, though."

Through the window into the back yard, Cameron could see one head then the other as the twins bounced on the trampoline, shrieking with glee.

"One thing I've noticed," Mom went on, "is that the God of the New Testament is much less harsh then the God of the Old Testament. The books of Leviticus and Deuteronomy spell out horrible repercussions for anyone who disobeyed God's law in even the smallest way."

Cameron angled his head as he looked at his mother. Could things really be about to change?

Mom focused on peeling potatoes. After a moment, she carried on. "Jesus upheld the law, but He pointed out so many things that turned society on its head back then. He said that thinking something was as bad as doing it." She glanced at Dad. "Even though I never slept with the minister of music from our church, I was tempted. I thought about it. And, in God's eyes, what I did was just as wrong as what your father did."

Dad's head jerked upright, his eyes riveted on Mom's.

"The Bible has a lot of interesting things to say, doesn't it?" Cameron said into the silence. "One of the things I've noticed lately is where Jesus said He didn't condemn people. He just asked that those who had not sinned be the first to cast stones."

Mom nodded as she stared at Dad. "You're right. God is much more willing to forgive than I've been. But that's about to change. I forgive you, Wilfred."

Dad slowly rose from his chair and took a few steps

toward Mom.

Looked like the first true step toward reconciliation. Cameron glanced at the clock on the microwave. "I'll get out of your hair now. I need to pick Alaina up in ten minutes."

Dad stretched both hands toward Mom and she grasped them, pulling him a little closer. Their eyes remained locked on each other's.

Cameron grinned. "Don't burn dinner. Don't forget the boys are outside." Not that anyone heard him or paid attention.

Mom hadn't come right out and said she was done making a big deal out of his divorce, but he was pretty sure that would come later, after she and Dad had got things squared away.

Gave him hope for his evening with Alaina. *Please, Lord, smooth over whatever the difficulty is. I believe You've brought her into my life, and we need You.*

Alaina spread the white linen napkin across her lap with trembling fingers. L'Aubergine. She'd heard of this restaurant since her return to Arcadia Valley two months back but had never come in. The atmosphere was every bit as romantic as Joanna and Evelyn had said.

The waiter had tucked them in front of a bay window overlooking the restaurant's herb garden. She could imagine coming here in winter with snow cloaking the garden, a fire crackling in the fireplace across the small dining alcove, and flickering candles between them. Even in the warmth and sunshine of an August evening, the space seemed private. Intimate.

Make-it-or-break-it-night. But how was she supposed to end things with him when he brought her to such a beautiful, expensive place? Maybe that was part of his plan.

She sneaked a peek at him. He looked so good. His short brown hair, just long enough to be soft under her fingertips. His clean-shaven jaw. His expressive brown eyes, looking down at the menu in his hands. Was he trembling? Or was that her imagination?

"Would you like the breaded zucchini sticks in marinara sauce for an appetizer?" he asked.

He was going all out. "That sounds good," she answered. "And the lamb chops look like a delicious entrée."

Cameron nodded. "I think I'll have the prime rib myself." He folded both heavy padded menus and set them at the end of the table.

The server took their orders and brought their drinks.

"Thanks for coming with me tonight, Alaina." Cameron reached across the table and covered her hands where they fidgeted with the heavy silverware.

"Thanks for asking me." Wow, this was just as awkward as the first time or two they'd gone out.

"My mom and dad are in my kitchen right now making up." He chuckled. "Or possibly making out."

"I'm glad." And she was.

Cameron's thumbs rubbed circles on the backs of Alaina's hands. Warmth trickled through her body. She loved this man. He loved her back. Didn't he? Surely he wasn't only looking for someone to fill the housekeeping gap in his household. But this awkwardness would remain until she spoke up.

"Cameron?"

The warmth in his brown eyes pierced her to her very soul. "Yes, sweetheart?"

"You said something the other day that got me thinking..."

Nothing in his demeanor changed. His hands on hers remained as warm as the expression on his face.

Alaina took a deep breath. "You said something about your home and your kitchen needing me. You seemed to think I would automatically be cooking dinner when I was at your house with the boys. I'm not exactly sure what you meant."

His jaw tensed slightly and his brows furrowed. "I love you, Alaina. I can't help but look forward to the day when you might become my wife. I told you from the beginning that I wasn't looking for a casual relationship."

"What are you looking for in a wife?" She tried to pull her hands away from his, but his grip intensified. Not so tightly she felt trapped, just that he wasn't letting go easily.

"You."

Alaina's heart hammered in her chest, all but blocking her ability to breathe. "What about me makes you think I'm wife material?"

"I'm not really sure what you're asking," he said slowly, his eyes searching hers.

She should have waited until they've eaten this delicious dinner, but her nerves were too fragile. Now she would either ruin it completely, or — please, God — her fears might be set to rest, and she could enjoy it.

"Do you think it's the wife's role to cook, clean, and do laundry? Do you want a wife who will stay home and make the household run smoothly as her sole job? Because I have a career, Cameron. I trained for it for four years, and I've worked in the field for another six since then. I love working with children, and I believe that's what God has called me to do."

"I see. You're concerned because it seems that's the kind of wife my mother is."

Alaina nodded then shook her head, looking down at the white tablecloth. "It's just the way you said it the other day that got me worried. I'm not sure I can live up to this ideal of yours, Cameron. I was raised differently. My parents expected my sister and me to get an education and not to be afraid to use it."

"I tried the other way once already," Cameron said softly. "And you know how well it turned out for me. I'm sure it wasn't the only thing wrong between Lisa and me. She never made a profession of faith in Jesus, either. She didn't care if she followed His standards or not so, long term, there was no way we were going to have a marriage that lasted fifty years."

Alaina peeked up at him through her lowered lashes. "I didn't pay enough attention to that with Garth, either. We would never have made it."

"I'm not a very good cook, Alaina. My sister can tell you that. My mom would be happy to tell you all my shortcomings." He chuckled. "Of course, I would love to have someone else put healthy and tasty meals on the table every night."

She managed to pull her hands away from his. "Then I guess I'm the wrong woman for you."

"Alaina?"

His soft voice, the way he said her name, the love shining in his eyes nearly undid her. Maybe she could try. Maybe, for him, it would be worth giving everything up.

"I tried that route. I tried to be the breadwinner and keep Lisa barefoot and pregnant. I wasn't interested in the things she wanted to do to be fulfilled. I wanted to prove... I don't know what I wanted to prove. All I know is that we didn't communicate, and a lot of that was my fault. I wasn't listening." Cameron reached across the table and lifted her chin with one finger. "I'm listening now. I'm listening to *you*."

Alaina sucked in her bottom lip as she met his gaze. "I'll be really honest. I'm not a very good cook, either. It seems my sister got all those genes. But I'm willing to learn how... with you. I'm willing to do almost anything so long as it is with you."

"I think that's the key, isn't it? Doing things together. Adjusting. Give-and-take on both sides."

"Being partners like that sounds pretty amazing, actually."

He lifted her hands, brought them to his lips, and kissed them. Her stomach fluttered, and she felt weak. If she'd been standing, her knees might've buckled out from underneath her. As it was, she swayed in her chair. Oh the things that man could do with his lips. Suddenly, she could hardly wait for more.

Chapter 25

C AMERON TOOK ALAINA'S HAND as they strolled out of the community center two months later. "Who knew cooking together could possibly be this much fun?"

She grinned up at him. "I know, right? My parents always made it look so much fun. Truth be told, my dad does even more of the cooking than Mom does."

"A man before his time." Cameron tucked Alaina close to his side.

Around them, the other couples from their cooking class climbed into their cars and drove away. Grady squeezed the horn on his Eos as he and Joanna pulled out of the parking lot. It was fun having his sister and brother-in-law in the same class. They'd shared a lot of laughs.

The last vestiges of twilight lingered in the western sky, and the nearly full moon already rode on the eastern horizon. "Want to go for a walk, sweetheart?"

"I'd love to. It's so still out here. So peaceful."

Cameron chuckled. "My parents should have the twins in bed before I can get back home."

"I think it's awesome that they're sticking around Arcadia Valley a bit longer. How is your dad finding working for Ben at Corinna's Cupboard?"

"Pretty well, actually. Max Martinez is paying him to do some renovation work to the old building. Dad seems to be handier than I ever knew about."

"And they're getting the counseling they need. It's great the Bible school gave them a leave of absence for one semester. Do you think they'll be ready to go back to England in January?"

"That's their plan." Cameron swallowed hard. Would there be a better moment? He'd been packing around the small box from Facets for two weeks now, but he kept losing his nerve at the last minute. "They'd like to be here for the wedding."

"Oh? Whose wedding?"

Cameron reached into his pocket then dropped on one knee.

Alaina's hands flew to cover her mouth as her eyes grew wide.

"Ours. If you'll marry me, that is. Alaina, I love you so much, and I don't see how my life could ever be complete without you in it. Will you be my wife?"

"Your... wife?"

His sweaty hands fumbled with the velvet box as he pried it open. He angled it so the rising moon glinted off the diamond. "Please, Alaina. Say you will. I know I come with a package deal, a pair of rambunctious twins who adore you. I can't promise you only sunny days and full moons, but I can promise you love. I can promise you a husband who wants to live his life rooted and grounded in God's love, so he can demonstrate that love to you every day as long as we both shall live."

"Cameron?" Her hands stroked his face, her thumbs gliding across his cheekbones. "My roots have been transplanted so many times, but no more. I know you're my forever love. I'll be glad to marry you."

He pulled the ring from its snug bed and slipped it onto her finger. Then he rose to his feet and wrapped one arm around her. "Do you like it? We can get a different one if you prefer."

She tilted her hand this way and that in the moonlight. "I think it's perfect," she breathed. "It's everything I ever wished for. And so are you."

"You always wanted to share your life with seven-year-old twins who like to put frogs in people's beds?"

"I admit I thought that might be ten years in my future," she said with a chuckle. "But I'm pretty fond of Evan and Oliver. We have many books to read before they sleep."

"Maybe someday we'll have another set of twins just like them." Cameron couldn't help teasing. "Fraternal twins run in my dad's family."

"I'm putting in my order for baby girls in that case." She slid both arms around his neck, tangling her fingers in the hair at his nape. "I love you, Cameron Kraus. Did you have any particular dates in mind?"

"You mean besides tomorrow?"

"I could get on board with that." Her lips parted.

Cameron closed his mouth over hers as every nerve ending in his body fired at the same time. "I talked to your boss about when you could get some time off work."

She tipped her head back and raised her eyebrows as she looked at him.

"She said the Grace Greenhouse kids program will be closed for two weeks over Christmas. Is that too soon?"

Alaina pulled his head down and whispered against his lips. "Not nearly soon enough."

Something else they agreed on. Cameron held the woman he loved close in his arms and kissed her. There was no way he wanted to leave any room for her to doubt the depth of his love.

Dear Reader

Do you share my passion for locally grown real food? No, I'm not as fanatical or fixated as many of the characters I write about, but gardening, cooking, and food processing comprise a large part of my non-writing life.

Whether you're new to the concept or a long-time advocate, I invite you to my website and blog at www.valeriecomer.com to explore God's thoughts on the junction of food and faith.

Please sign up for my monthly newsletter while you're there! My gift to all subscribers is *Peppermint Kisses*, a short story set in the Farm Fresh Romance series. Joining my list is the best way to keep tabs on my food/farm life as well as contests, cover reveals, deals, and news about upcoming books. I welcome you!

Enjoy this Book?

Please leave a review at any online retailer or reader site. Letting other readers know what you think about *Rooted in Love: An Arcadia Valley Romance* helps them make a decision and means a lot to me. Thank you!

If you haven't read any of my other books, may I suggest the six-book Farm Fresh Romances? The first story is *Raspberries and Vinegar*.

Keep reading for the first chapter of *The Sound of Romance* by Danica Favorite, the next book in the multi-author Arcadia Valley Romance series.

The Sound

of Romance

— an Arcadia Valley Romance —

DANICA FAVORITE

Chapter One

C ole Anderson had been in love with Allie Bigby for just about ever. To some, it might sound like an exaggeration, but from the moment he laid eyes on her in elementary school, he knew that someday he was going to make Allie Bigby his wife. When he told his best friend Peter Houston, Peter had scoffed saying a third-grader would never waste his time on someone in a baby class, because Allie was a first-grader. But even then, Cole held firm to that belief. He'd just kept it to himself for all these years.

Except for a few failed attempts at getting her attention in high school, Cole had never let on how deeply he cared for Allie. He'd always hoped that someday, they'd find a way to be together. Which was hard to do when Allie never seemed to know he existed.

When he saw her working the register at Gas N' Shop,

after him having been gone for more than ten years, his heart skipped a beat. No ring on the finger, and from what his sister-in-law had told him, no guy in the picture at all. He'd just hoped for a little more time before being faced with his childhood crush. Even so, he hadn't expected the memories of Allie to come to mind so readily.

"How can I help you?" Allie said with the dimpled smile he'd never been able to get out of his mind.

"I'm looking for…"

What had he come in there for? Cole looked around frantically. Gum? No. Mints? No. Dried beef sticks? No. Tacky Christmas knickknacks? No. Woman with a crying baby on the other side of the store? That triggered something.

"I need a wife," he blurted.

Allie gaped at him, just as she had in high school when his grand attempt at asking her to Homecoming had crashed and burned. He'd been certain that if she could see just how much he was willing to do for her, she'd realize what a great guy he was.

How was he supposed to know that singing "You've Lost That Loving Feeling" to a girl only resulted in a date in the movie, *Top Gun*? Maybe, if she'd been as airplane crazy as he'd been at the time, she'd have seen the old movie and known what to do. But that was beside the point.

Had he just told Allie Bigby that he was looking for a wife?

"I'm afraid we're fresh out of wives," she said, shaking her head. "Actually, I'm pretty sure we stopped selling females here about twenty years ago, when they converted the sale barn to the Gas N' Shop. And even then, I don't think they sold humans."

Was she trying to be funny or was she being serious? It was hard to tell with Allie because every time he tried to talk to her, everything he said came out so jumbled that she always walked away shaking her head. Like she was doing now.

"No, wait. I... that's not what I meant. I need something for my wife."

Oh no. He didn't have a wife. What was he saying? Why couldn't he string more than two words together in a sentence when he was around her?

"Sorry. I meant my brother's wife. Jess sent me. The..." He took a deep breath.

What was wrong with him? A simple errand for his sister-in-law and he couldn't remember what it was. Why did Allie Bigby make him so discombobulated? Recognition dawned on Allie's face.

"She was supposed to pick up some things from me earlier, is that what you mean?"

"Yes." Cole let out a long sigh. "I can't believe I forgot what it was. Some kind of salve she needed for the baby's diaper rash."

Diaper rash. One more inappropriate topic to be discussing with the woman of his dreams. But surely Allie knew what he was there for, and that it was meant for diaper rash. After all, Allie was the one who made the stuff. From what Jessica had told him, she was a real whiz at creating homemade items out of lavender.

"Cole Anderson." She said his name slowly as she shook her head. "I heard you were here for a visit."

"You remember me?"

Allie stared at him. "How could I not? You made high school miserable for me."

Yeah, so on the scale of one to ten of the world's greatest love stories, he was pretty sure this response wouldn't even give it a zero. He tried consoling himself by saying that at least she remembered him, but from the look on her face, he'd rather she didn't.

Could he get a do-over on this whole pursuing Allie thing?

"I'm sorry, I don't really remember that part." It was the best he could come up with on such short notice. Especially because he thought that he'd been the one humiliated, not Allie.

Allie gave him a smile that he didn't think she meant in a nice way.

"Oh, but I do. I know you supposedly had a crush on me back then, but you had some funny ways of showing a girl you liked her. So please, do me a favor. Steer clear of me while you're here." Allie reached under the counter and then handed him a box.

"Here's the salve. Take it and go before something terrible happens."

From the way she talked, Cole supposed he should have been grateful she didn't hand him a restraining order. It was slightly mortifying that his attempts at getting her to go out with him in high school were such a bad memory for her.

He'd envisioned that his reunion with Allie would be a little more... joyous. Or at least the same kind of reunion he'd had with his old friends when he ran into them since his return to Arcadia Valley. When he stopped by El Corazon, his favorite Mexican restaurant, he was immediately greeted by his old friend Javier, who'd given him dinner on the house because it had been so long since they'd seen each other.

Several of their other old friends had stopped in, and it was almost like a reunion. Allie's brother, Andrew, had also been one of Cole's good friends, and he'd come by. Though maybe Cole should have gotten the hint when he'd asked about Allie, and Andrew had abruptly changed the subject.

As Cole turned to leave, he nearly ran into a short woman with dark hair, who clearly had something on her mind.

"I knew it!"

The woman yanked the box out of Cole's hand, and held it in the air. "You *are* selling your lavender stuff out of here. Just wait until I tell Dan."

As she was speaking, the door had opened and an older, balding man stepped in. "Tell me what?"

"Even though you've asked her not to, Allie has been selling her lavender products here at the Gas N' Shop. I just watched this man get some from her."

Cole glanced over at Allie, who looked even more angry than she had when she'd talked to him.

"I didn't sell anything," Allie said. "No money changed hands. You can check the security camera if you don't believe me."

At least Cole had a chance to help her out of this mess. "It's true. I didn't give her any money. I was just picking this up for my sister-in-law. She already paid for it."

Instead of looking grateful, Allie looked like she wanted to throttle him.

"That's still selling," the woman said, smiling like she'd won a big prize.

"I didn't sell it to her." Allie turned to Dan. "It was just a favor to a friend. A gift. How many times have you left things here for friends to pick up? Just the other day, you had me give those flies you made to Stan Baumgardner. I made the salve for Jess, but I didn't have time to drop it off at her house earlier. I was going to run it to her when I got off," Allie looked over at the clock on the wall. "Which was supposed to be fifteen minutes ago."

Dan nodded slowly. "Who is this guy, then?"

Allie gave him a look, like she wanted him to stay out of it. "Her brother-in-law. I don't know why she sent him, but it doesn't really matter. The point is, it was just something I made for her friend, who sent someone to pick it up rather than wait for me to come by."

"But you're still wasting company time," the nasty woman said, crossing her arms over her chest. "I'll bet you don't have those reports done."

"Actually, I do." Allie walked back around the counter and pulled out a folder from underneath. "I have all the stocking done for the day, and I went through the order list and updated it, and-"

"Enough," Dan said. "I get the picture. But you know how I feel about you conducting personal business from the store."

Shaking her head, Allie let out a long sigh. "I do. Honestly, since the last time you talked to me about this, I haven't brought my work here. This was just a favor for a friend whose baby has a miserable diaper rash. It was an emergency."

"Emergency or not, friends are still personal business," the woman said.

Cole wanted to smack the smirk off her face. Why wasn't Allie defending herself more strongly? If she wouldn't, then he would. He turned to her. "I know it's hard for you to understand what it must be like to have friends, but you should give Allie a break. She's the nicest person I know, and she doesn't deserve to be talked to like this."

"It's fine, Cole. Just go home, and I'll sort this out. Nadia just misunderstood what was going on, and that's that. But as she has rightfully pointed out, this is a place of business, and we all need to get back to work."

Allie turned to go back to the counter, but Nadia stopped her. "I'm here now, you can just go home. We'll call you if we decide you can come back to work."

"What are you saying?" Allie's voice was quiet, and Cole hated the defeated tone it had taken.

Surely they weren't going to fire her over something so silly?

Cole took another step forward. "You can't just leave her hanging like that. You haven't given her due process, and if you're going to fire her, then you need to give her her last paycheck."

Nadia nodded, and for the first time, she looked almost like she was going to be reasonable. "You're right. Let me go into the back and write her a check. That way she knows for sure she's fired."

That wasn't exactly what he'd been aiming for, especially since Allie looked like she was about to cry. But really, was working for such an awful person the best she could do with her life?

"It's a terrible job anyway," Cole said. "Allie doesn't need this job."

Allie shot him a glare that made him want to be sick. Apparently, defending her had not been his brightest idea.

"Actually, I do need this job. It's a great job, and I'm happy to have it. Cole doesn't speak for me, just as you don't speak for Dan. He owns the place, not you."

Turning to Dan, Allie said, "You know I'm a good worker. I come in early, I stay late, I cover whatever shifts you need. Yes, I made a mistake, and I'm sorry. It didn't cost us any business, since no customers have come in this entire space of time. I can assure you, it won't happen again."

At least Dan looked like he was thinking about her words. He nodded slowly, as if she had made several good points. And Cole would admit that she had. Probably better points than he had. He should have done what Allie asked, and stayed out of it.

"How many times has she said that?" Nadia said, glaring at Dan. "You promoted me to assistant manager to make this store more profitable. She's a distraction from where this business needs to go. This isn't the first time we've had to talk to her about her many failings. If you can't man up and do the right thing, then you're going to need to find another assistant manager."

Was this woman serious?

Apparently, she was. Because Dan looked completely and utterly defeated. "I'm sorry, Allie."

Allie nodded slowly. "I know you are." Then she looked

over Nadia and shook her head. "It didn't have to be like this. I really wish we could have worked together in a cooperative manner for the good of our community. I'm sorry you didn't feel the same way."

Her words didn't appear to affect Nadia at all. "I'll just go get your check."

"Thanks." Then Allie turned to Dan. "I hope you know what you're doing, because you and I both know this isn't right."

He didn't respond, and Cole was glad. Mostly because Cole wasn't sure he could continue keeping his mouth shut in light of this injustice.

Still, he had to say something to encourage her. "It'll be all right. You'll find a new job. A better job."

Allie spun and glared at him. "Since apparently, I no longer work here, I also no longer have to be nice to the customers. I know you think you mean well, but you've done enough damage. If you want to help me, do as I asked and go home. And never bother me again."

As reunions went, this definitely was not what Cole had been expecting.

Coming back to Arcadia Valley was only supposed to be a temporary pit stop over the holidays until Cole could figure out what he wanted to do with his life now that the Army had determined he was unfit for service. Thanks to a training jump gone wrong, his back was too messed up for him to pass his physicals.

For a brief moment, he'd actually thought that maybe he could find a way to start over in Arcadia Valley. His brother, his uncle, old friends, and seeing Allie again. He hadn't been able to win her heart in high school, and now, that goal seemed farther away than ever.

Maybe it was a sign that he really and truly did have to move on.

His life was basically ruined. And judging by the way she'd glared at him on his way out, she thought hers was too. The difference was, somebody as pretty, healthy, smart, and talented as Allie had a lot of options. No one grew up wanting to work at the Gas N' Shop.

He really had been trying to help. But maybe, this was all a blessing in disguise. He'd help Allie find a better job, and hopefully, in the process, figure out his own life as well.

The Sound of Romance

is available through online retailers.
Find out more at
ArcadiaValleyRomance.com

Author Biography

Valerie Comer lives where food meets faith in her real life, her fiction, and on her blog and website. She and her husband of over 35 years farm, garden, and keep bees on a small farm in Western Canada, where they grow and preserve much of their own food.

Valerie has always been interested in real food from scratch, but her conviction has increased dramatically since God blessed her with four delightful granddaughters. In this world of rampant disease and pollution, she is compelled to do what she can to make these little girls' lives the best she can. She helps supply healthy food — local food, organic food, seasonal food — to grow strong bodies and minds.

Valerie is a *USA Today* bestselling author and a two-time Word Award winner. She writes engaging characters, strong communities, and deep faith into her green clean romances.

To find out more, visit her website at www.valeriecomer.com, where you can read her blog, explore her many links, and sign up for her email newsletter to download the free short story: *Peppermint Kisses: A (short) Farm Fresh Romance 2.5*. You can also use this QR code to access the newsletter sign-up.

Made in the USA
Lexington, KY
11 October 2018